More Than Anything

MORE SERIES BOOK TWO

S. VAN HORNE

COLLABORATIONS WITH:
MARY B. MOORE AND M.L. RODRIGUEZ

Dedication

To my amazing husband, Lee. Thank you for all the love and support you have given me during this journey. I couldn't do it without you and I'm blessed that you are along with me for this incredible ride. You are the most amazing husband and father. I feel so blessed that God gave you to me.

I love you, One More Time xoxo.

Lee and Sonya – Wedding day May 19, 2000

P.S. Eve, Neil's yours.

More Than Anything

At twenty-seven, Sara Reyes had tried to stay hidden working for Seal Security. It was a chance for her to be protected and her loved ones to be safe—until the phone call . . .

At twenty-eight, Neil Shields had felt like things were falling into place. Now that his sister was back at home, he decided nothing would stop him from going after his fiery redhead goddess—until she ran . . .

Now, stakes are high to find out what Sara's hiding and why there are people after her. Will Neil ever find Sara and express how she means more than anything to him?

Note From Author

PTSD is very close to my heart, and I wanted to bring more awareness that people suffer from this daily, along with depression. I hope you take a moment and do some research on PTSD to help understand how you can help someone who is suffering from these . . . even if that someone is yourself.

I hope you enjoy Neil and Sara's story.

With much love,

Sonya

P.S. There's a character in this book that's from another book. Coleman is from the Mary B Moore's Providence Series. Part of Neil's POV in Chapter Seven of this book is from her book *Until Forever* that we collaborated on. Chapter Eleven will be in her *Redemption* book —Amity series that's due out in early 2017. Make sure you go and check it out. Our characters will be visiting each other and working together. Also, they'll be vacationing together soon. So, keep an eye out for that.

Additionally, the Epilogue and Bonus was written by ML Rodriguez. Her character, Jake, is part of her La Flor series, Leap of Faith and Imperfectly Beautiful. Make sure you go and read those books so you know who Jake is and her other characters. They will be making future appearances in my book, and we plan on collaborating on a book together in the future with some of our characters.

*The chapters that were collaborated will be marked with *** under the chapter heading. *

P.P.S. When you get to Rebecca's POV please note IT IS NOT A PRESENT POV! These are her journal entries and are her thoughts at that time when she wrote in her book. It's important to remember this as you read this story.

P.P.S.S. A quick special thanks to KC Lynn, K. Langston, C.M. Steele, Elena M. Reyes, and Cassia Brightmore for allowing me to use your names in a chapter of my book. Please make sure you go and check out these amazing authors. I adore their books and am so honored they allowed me to add them to my book <3 Their links will be at the back under more authors to check out.

Now . . . On to Neil and Sara's story . . .

Prologue

NEIL

I STARE AT THE JOURNAL in my hand and read the first page again.

Dear Journal:

I've never done this before. Never had to write my feelings or thoughts. I've always been able to express myself openly. Now, I'm no longer able to do that. I'm no longer able to be anything. Today, I became a number . . . a statistic . . . a ghost of what I was. I have no clue what will become of me. Where I will go? Or who I will become? I no longer have anyone but the two people I'm told I have to trust. I have to give them my life to keep safe, and after what happened today, I don't know if I can.

I thought since I finally found my one, I would finally get the family I have wanted for the past year. I was finally going to have that house, dog, husband, children, flowers in the front yard with an amazing garden in the back that we eat from . . . I thought I had it all. I was wrong, God, was I so wrong.

Now . . . now I'm just a nobody in a sea of people that will never know who I truly am inside. Maybe this writing thing will help me remember the real me, or maybe it will make me want to just end it all because there's nothing really left for me here anymore.

-Rebecca

The feeling of pain goes through my chest at the thought that I'm reading a journal of someone that might have killed themself. Sitting back in my chair, I close my eyes and try to figure out why someone would leave this in my office. If she is still alive, I'm sure she's searching everywhere for it because God knows, I would be if I were them.

One

Rebecca

Present . . .

DEEP BREATH . . . YOU GOT THIS, Becca. Just a few hours, and then you can write in your journal and get the feelings out. Just hold it together . . .

Sara

I glance around Len's backyard and smile at the happiness that fills the air. I've always wanted a family that could come together and celebrate the small joys that life brings. I almost had that at one point in my life, but it was ripped from my hands before I could even grasp it. A pang of sadness and fear flood my body, but I push it away, not wanting it to take over this brief moment of bliss.

I peek out of the corner of my eye to the left and find Neil watching me. He's the hottest guy I've ever laid eyes on. The moment I met him three years ago, I thought I would faint from just how damn good looking he was. He seemed like a stuck-up asshole, with the way he wouldn't say shit to me. All he did was glare like I took the prize out of his cereal box on Sunday morning while changing the channel from his favorite cartoons.

But it slowly started changing, and I realized that he just wasn't interested in me, and was very protective of his sister. I'm not one to open up and tell people my problems; as a matter of fact, nobody knows about my problems right now. I'm afraid to reveal the truth, of them finding out just how much trouble I can bring to their family.

I know I should be more open about it, but the detectives assured me that my file is closed tight, and that it couldn't be tampered with. That's the only thing saving me right now from Neil finding out about my past. At first, I was scared of what he would find out when he did my background check for Seal Security. But nothing came up, and that was a sigh of relief.

Then, there was that one night at the lake that I can't get out of my mind. It was the best night of my life, and I wanted to reach out and grab what Neil was offering with both hands. But my past stopped me from doing that. So, for now I live through my memories and try to keep him at arm's length even though he's doing everything in his power to change that.

The sound of laughter snaps me back into the present, and I notice pink and blue balloons rising in the air. I'm confused for a brief moment until I hear the word "twins." A huge grin spreads across my face at the thought of Dante having three kids in diapers, one of which is a girl.

That man is an alpha to the max at times, so I know that

little one is going to end up hating her daddy when she gets older due to his overprotectiveness.

The sound of a phone catches me off guard, and I realize it's mine. I reach in my purse and pull it out to see who could be calling me. Everyone that would call is here, so it has to be the call service for Seal Security. With me as the main admin for the front, all calls come to me when we aren't in the office.

I glance at the screen and freeze once I see the name and number.

This can't be happening.

He said he wouldn't call unless it's an emergency. I'm not sure if I want to answer it.

"*Habibti*, you okay?" Neil asks, coming up to me.

"I need to take this," I say and rush off to the side of the house to take the phone in private.

"Hello," I answer, my voice trembling softly, afraid of what he might say.

"Sara?" a voice I know so well on the other end questions.

"Yes, this is she."

"They know, Sara. I need you to get here as soon as you can. We've got to get you to safety." I close my eyes at the words; one of my biggest fears is becoming reality.

After gathering enough strength, I make my way back and spot Neil and Dante. "I have to go. Please tell Len I'll call her later." I rush out before turning and running to the front of the house. Neil runs after me, shouting my name, but I quickly say something over my shoulder without stopping.

The life I know, the life I've come to build, is no more. All I can do, all I *must* do, is leave. They've found me, and in order to keep those I love safe, I need to run without turning back.

NEIL

I glance, yet again, at the redheaded goddess that has been on my mind from the moment we met three years ago. During that first meeting, I didn't mean to glare at her the whole time, but I was trying to figure out why I wanted to pick her up, throw her over my shoulder, and never share her with the world. It bothered me that she had that much power over me.

Then, I realized that the only reason I would feel that with her was because she was my one. After that, I tried everything to get her to notice me, short of just announcing that I liked her and wanted her. Nothing seemed to work, and right when I was about to just take that plunge, my sister came up missing, and that stopped everything.

It isn't a secret that I'm a protective ass when it comes to my sister. So when she vanished the night of my company party, I felt like I failed her. After a few weeks of her missing, I knew that after she was found, only then would I go after Sara, and nothing would stop me from having her.

That night at the lake was the most amazing night of my life. I had never felt perfection like I did when I made love to her for the first time or the times that followed that night. But the following morning, I woke to an empty bed, abandoned and furious. When I stormed downstairs, she acted like she didn't even know me, and that made me even angrier. I'm not one to blow up in public, so I bit my lip and decided to wait until we had a second alone.

But, that second never came.

After Adams was killed, it took a while to get things back to normal, and by then I was over the anger. Now, I'm trying everything to get back to that one night we had. So far, I haven't made much leeway.

The sound of Sara's phone snaps me out of my thoughts. When she glances down to look at her screen, she turns pale, and I immediately rush over to her side.

"*Habibti*, you okay?"

"I need to take this," she states, her voice trembling with fear, and rushes off to the side of the house. Before I can follow, Ghost steps up besides me and stops me from intruding on her call.

As he holds me back, I see her listening intently to the person on the phone. Whatever they say has her turning even more pale. I swear I can feel her fear radiating from her body. I don't know who is on the other line, but right when I'm about to march over there and snatch the phone from her to find out who the fuck it is. She hangs up before I can do just that, and glances over at us. She quickly makes her way over, her eyes showing nothing but pure, unadulterated fear.

"I have to go. Please tell Len I'll call her later," she whispers, and then turns and rushes to her car.

It takes me a moment to process her words before I'm hot on her tail, chasing her.

"Sara, wait a minute. What the fuck is going on?" I yell.

"I don't have time to explain, Neil. I have an emergency. I'll call later," she tosses over her shoulder without stopping.

She's in her car and has it started before I can reach her.

Just as I get close enough, she glances toward me with tears streaming down her face. So much hurt is coming through her beautiful green eyes that it has me stopping in my tracks, preventing me from opening her car door. Instead, my chest rises and falls fast, and my eyes silently beg her to come to me.

"I'm sorry, Neil. I never wanted you to know. Please, let me go," she whispers out of her window that's barely down.

"Never," I growl out between clenched teeth. Before I can open her door, she flips the lock and shakes her head sadly.

"Goodbye, Neil. If you remember anything, remember this: you always made me feel as if I was so much more than what I thought I would ever be," she states with a soft smile as the tears just keep streaming down. She pulls out of the driveway without a backwards glance.

I stand there, shocked at the words she just spoke, watching as her car fades down the road. I vow in that moment that she isn't getting away from me that easily.

Furious, hurt, and determined, I turn and storm back into the house to let the others know that I have to go. I have to find Sara and get to the bottom of this once and for all.

It's time she sees the beast within me. The beast that will weather any storm her past can bring. Because nothing will stop me from showing her just how much more she really means to me.

Two

Rebecca

Ten years earlier . . .

I WALK INTO MY APARTMENT, and instantly feel the relief of the air conditioning that has been on since five this morning when I left for work. My shoes are the first to go, then I walk into the bedroom to get a change of clothes so I can take a quick shower. Arturo will be home soon and the plans are to meet his brother, Mauricio, and his best friend, Rupert, for drinks. This is our Friday night ritual, and I desperately need it after working in the hot factory all day.

Stepping into the shower, I let the hot water soak into my muscles. I had a shit day, and the heat didn't help. We had an order of five thousand blades that got trashed. This puts us behind by at least three weeks now. I'm not looking forward to the overtime that's going to have to happen to get this order out. Don't get me wrong—the money will be good, but it will take away from the time I have with Arturo, and we don't get much since he's been working long hours here lately.

As my muscles slowly relax from the hot water, I reflect on how Arturo and I met. It was a very low point in my life. It was right after I finished my junior year of high school. I had enough credits to graduate my junior year, but I was missing one gym credit. My school had a program that I could get that credit at the local college during the summer, then I could work my whole senior year, and I would be able to walk with them. Two weeks into my summer class, my world was shaken; my parents were killed due to a drunk driver who decided to drive home after a bender at the local bar.

I had nobody left in this world. Being that I was an only child and my parents were only children, we didn't have family for me to go and live with. My parents were what you would consider hermits and didn't have many friends. I was staying with my neighbor while filing for the ability to just live on my own. Since I didn't have to finish school, and knowing I would be seventeen soon, I knew if I could just prove to the system that I could be an adult, then I wouldn't have to go into foster care. I decided to file paperwork to become emancipated, which then would make me an adult, even though I would be under the age of eighteen.

One day I was running late to class at the college because of a meeting that ran late with the lawyer, and I ended up literally smacking into a guy and hurting my ankle. That was the last straw. I sat on my ass in the middle of the sidewalk, sobbing out my pain of all that had happened over the last few months. The stranger ended up holding me, and telling me that everything would be okay. That was the start of the relationship that has been going on for a year now, and led to me moving in with him after I was finally granted emancipation.

Arturo has been my rock since that moment. He supports what I want to do and shows me just what it means to be loved by a man. A lot of people look down at our relationship since I'm only seventeen and he's twenty-one, but they don't understand that we're in love, and that I'm no longer considered a minor in the law's eyes. He also waited to make love to me until I was ready. That wasn't until only a few months ago. I feel extremely lucky to have him in my life.

The sound of the front door snaps me out of my thoughts and has me peeking out from behind the curtain.

"Baby."

"In here," I yell out.

I watch him walk in and see his sexy smirk play out on his face. I know what's coming before he even says it. "Don't even think about it." Warning him does no good because it's a daily thing with him.

"You getting wet for me, baby?" This causes me to roll my eyes and slam the curtain shut. But I should have known better than to think this would stop him from being his pervy self.

"Because if you are, then I'm game for taking care of any ache you may be having." I hear him dropping stuff on the counter and know that my shower alone isn't going to happen.

"Arturo, we don't have time! We're supposed to meet the guys in an hour."

The curtain jerks open, and he's standing there in nothing but his sexy smirk. I shake my head and step back into the wall.

"We always got time, baby." And with that he enters the

shower, crowds me against the wall, and shuts up any protests I had.

"Another!" Mauricio screams out at the bartender.

It's safe to say we are all drunk. I shouldn't be drinking, but knowing the bouncer and bartender helps on Friday nights. After we binged on tacos, which we all have a very unhealthy obsession with, we headed to the local bar and started drinking beer. Not to mention the shots of Patron on the side we did as well.

"A toast! To friends . . ." Rupert starts but is interrupted by Arturo when he jumps up and holds his arms in the air.

"Wait . . . I have something to say." He takes a deep breath and then turns toward me. While reaching into his pants pocket, he gives me a smirk. "Becs, you know you're my angel, and I'm so damn blessed you ran into me that day. I can't imagine my life without you." It's then I notice the bar is quiet and everyone is looking at us. I also realize that this is the moment I've been praying for since we moved in together. "Showers haven't been the same since you moved in. I need to make sure I get them for the rest of my life. So, will you marry me?"

Tears are forming in my eyes as I try to see past them and watch as the man I love drunkenly drops to one knee and holds up a simple diamond ring to me. I can't answer, so I just nod my head and hold my hand out. After he places the ring on my finger, I jump into his arms and realize the place is cheering for us.

"Well, little sister, I have to tell you. I would've been the better choice, but I'm super excited you're joining our family." Mauricio grabs me out of his brother's arms and hugs me.

"Way to go, man. Lock that shit down!" Rupert slaps Arturo on the back. "Now, a toast! To the two best people I know, other than this jerk next to me, Bec and Arturo! To many years of happiness and taco Fridays!" We all slam the shot back and laugh.

"Let's go home," I whisper into Arturo's ear.

"We're out of here." My hand is snagged as he tosses over his shoulder, "you have a key. Give us an hour."

Giggling, I wave over my shoulder and head out into the night with the love of my life. I look at my now-fiancé and smile. We have such an amazing life ahead of us, and I'm looking forward to seeing where it leads.

NEIL

Just a few more days.

Glancing to my left, I see my bags packed against my closet. I'm excited to start the new chapter in my life. Never did I think I would become a Navy Seal, but that's what the future is holding for not only me, but for my best friend, Dante, too.

Tonight, I'll be telling my family that I'll be heading off. They keep asking me what college I applied to, but I kept telling them that I wanted to have a family dinner and announce my plans to everyone at one time. Dante's telling his family tonight too. I'm worried about how my sister is going to react. She knows the plan as she overheard it, but I know it's hitting her hard.

My family consists of my parents, sister, and grandma. We're from Kansas City, Missouri, however we lived in Oak Harbor, Washington for a short amount of time. Well, my parents, sister, and I did. My Pa died while we were there, so my sister ended up moving back to live with OPG, Old Plain Grandma, until I graduated high school, and we moved back a few weeks ago. The best part is that my best friend from Washington and his family ended up moving with us. We sort of combined our families, and now we do everything together. We're super close, and honestly, I'm not sure how I'm going to live away from them. The only thing that's comforting is that Dante's joining me on this journey.

I've had friends ask why I wanted to join the Military. It's simple. I feel it's my duty to serve my country like those before us. It's like this draw for me to do something bigger for my country. One night I brought it up with Dante, and he felt the same. After taking the ASVAB—Armed Services Vocational Aptitude Battery, which is a test they give you to determine if you can join the military—and doing all we had to do to sign, both of us were offered to do something even bigger for our country. To become a Navy Seals. We thought long and hard for three days before we decided this is where we wanted to be and signed on the dotted line. Now, we have to tell our families . . . *Fuck my life.*

"What has you thinking so hard over there, big bro?" The sound of my sister's voice has me snapping my head in her direction.

"Dinner."

"You plan on telling everyone?" It's barely a whisper, but it's there.

"Yeah, squirt. I know it has been hard for you to keep it to yourself, and I'm grateful you did. You going to be okay?"

"Can I ask you something?" She takes a seat on my bed, then scoots over to me and snuggles down next to me.

I nod and wait to hear what she's going to ask. She's a loose cannon, so I question what she's going to come up with. Either it's going to be deep, or it's going to be one of those *what the hell* moments.

"Are you scared?"

I take a few moments to think her question over. Am I scared? Part of me is, and part of me is excited. This will be hard to explain. I know she's worried about the dangers of the job, and honestly, I would be stupid to say I'm not worried. But I don't want my family to know this is a possibility. I've always been honest with my sister, but I'm wondering if I should tell her the truth. I decided to just lay it out there, and hope for the best.

"What would I be scared of, squirt? War? Death? Seeing things I won't ever get out of my mind? Yeah, I could be scared of those things, but that isn't going to help me while I'm over there. I have to trust that my brothers will have my back, and that no matter what is seen, I have family and friends here at home to come back to. Also, I have a country that I feel I need to defend, and be there for. To give back for all it has given to us."

"Okay." It's whispered so softly that I almost missed it. Her next words hit my heart and make me hold her close. "Just come home to me. I can't live without my brother, Neil."

"I'll do my best, Len."

"And bring Dante back to us, too." She pokes me in the

side. "Now, let's go to dinner."

As we head to the door, I take a deep breath and get my mind together. If I thought that was hard, I know I haven't faced just how hard it was going to be to tell my parents and OPG.

"You're doing what?" The yelling of my mom's voice has me dropping my head into my hands and taking a deep breath. I knew she wasn't going to like this, but I didn't think she would scream at the top of her lungs in a five-star restaurant.

"Mom. Please. Voice."

"Don't Mom me, Neil Anthony Shields! You just told me you're not only joining the Navy, but you're going to be a Seal. And you want me to be calm?" she shrieks. I peek out from behind my hands and scan the restaurant and see people looking over with smirks on their faces. *Assholes.*

"Mom, I love you. I get you're worried . . ." and that's all I got out before she starts her rant again about not understanding what a mother's worry really is like.

"Constance, enough," OPG says quietly, then turns toward me. I brace because everyone in the family knows that when she speaks, you listen and follow. Plain and simple. "Why?"

It only takes a moment to get my thoughts together because I have to explain this right, or they will never get it.

"My country means everything to me, like my family. I feel like I need to be something bigger. I feel like I can make a difference, and the way I can do that is by giving back. If it wasn't for those before me, who fought for the rights that we take advantage of this day, then where would we really be? I need this. I need to do more, and this is my chance to do just that. And I'll be honest, I need my family to support this choice and be with me through it," I look at my mom as I state the last sentence.

"Good. We have your back, and we'll support you. Just make sure when the women flock to you, use your mind and use condoms. We don't need a dependa in this family," OPG says as she sips her beer.

"How do you know what a dependa is, Mom?" Pops questions, a look of horror flashing across his face at the realization that she knows the word. Honestly, I'm shocked too.

"Don't give me that look. I know what a dependa is, and have seen a few in my time. Did you forget that we have family that served, Anthony?" Her voice carries from our table and has people looking over at us.

"Wait, what does that mean?" Squirt pipes up from next to me.

"It's when a person is after a military member for the benefits the military gives them. So many will trap a military member so they can get health care, housing, and the list goes on. It's a very shameful and disgusting thing. Over the years, the term dependa was placed on those type of people," OPG explains.

"People really do that?" Glancing over, I see the disgust on Len's face at the thought. But OPG is right—it happens so much in the military, and it's a sad situation.

"Yeah it does, squirt."

"So, Neil, make sure you cover your submarine before you dive into the depths of anyone," OPG states loudly, which causes my mom to choke on the drink of water she was just taking and has my sister shaking with laughter.

I slowly start sinking into my chair trying to hide from the stares that are still on us.

"Jesus, Mom. No more beer."

"The day you take my beer from me is the day that I bend you over my knee and give you the spanking that you should have gotten at a young age. Now, where's that waitress? I need another." And just like that, she has turned the conversation light again. She looks over at me and winks, knowing what she was doing.

I look around the table as everyone weighs in on how Pops should have been spanked more as a child, and realize that what I'm about to do is for them. To allow them to continue doing just this. I just pray that one day I'll be able to rejoin them around the table.

Sara

Four months later . . .

I look around my new apartment and take a deep breath. The notifications on my phone sound, and I cringe, not wanting to see who it is. Ever since I got to Kansas City, I try to avoid my phone or even going outside. Detective Conti has been telling me that I need to pretend and act normal, but I just don't think it's going to happen anytime soon. Looking down at the screen, I see a text from one of the girls I met on campus.

The college life never appealed to me much, but the

detectives said I had to blend in as much as I can. Being eighteen and new in the area, the only way to make me look like I belong would be enrolling into college. The ping of my phone reminds me that I had a message waiting for me.

Len: *Hey girl, want to get together for coffee? My brother just announced to the family a big secret and I need some time away from them to vent.*

I take a moment and try to decide if I want to do this. Glancing out the window, I see it's still early and there's a Starbucks down the street from my apartment. Maybe she wouldn't mind walking back with me if I do it.

Me: *Starbucks down the street from me? I want to be back before dark if that's okay.*
Len: *Done. I'm bringing my gang with me. Julia and Ashley are going to love you.*

Shit! I was hoping it was just her and me, but I couldn't get that lucky.
Deep breaths, Sara. Deep breaths.
After a few moments to get over that it won't be just us, I head out and hope that making these friends won't end up like the last ones I had.

Three

Sara

Seven years later . . .

"NEXT WEEK, MAKE SURE YOU have your essays handed in on time. If you do not have them turned in, then it will be twenty percent off your midterm grade," Professor Smith yells at us as we get our belongings together.

I'm excited that this is my last year of college. I'm getting my graduate in business management. I started college thinking I wanted to do social studies, but after three years I decided it wasn't for me and switched. Now, after seven years of college work, I'm finally almost done and going to walk across the stage.

I step outside, and the cold hits my face and takes my breath away. That's the one thing I haven't able to get used to when it comes to the Midwest: the cold weather. Even though I've lived here now for seven years, I don't think I could ever get used to negative digits and snow that falls. The first time I saw the snow, I was excited—that lasted all but a day when I saw what happens when people walk or drive on the beautiful white stuff. The feeling of wind going through you no matter how many clothes you have on? Yeah . . . it isn't something I'll ever get used to.

It takes me a few minutes to adjust and wipe the tears that fall down my face from the wind. I start to walk when I spot someone at the end of the sidewalk that I haven't seen in five years. Panic sets in, and I'm afraid that this means I've been found. He swore he wouldn't contact me again unless it was desperately needed.

I see him shaking his head and nods at the cafeteria on campus, then he turns and heads that way. After taking a few deep breaths to calm my thoughts, I follow him. It takes me a few moments after entering to find him in a corner away from most of the crowd. I make my way over to him and slide into the seat across from him slowly.

"Sara."

"Detective Conti."

"Sara, deep breath, girl. It isn't what you're thinking. I just wanted you to know that the final deposit from the trust fund has been done. This is the last time it will happen, and I wanted to make sure you understood that. Sara, it's been seven years; it's time to live your life. You're graduating this year. Make friends and think about starting a family. If they were going to find you, they would've found you by now." He reaches out and rubs the top of my hands that are sitting on the table, turning white from the strain of holding them together so tightly.

"It isn't as easy as you're making it sound. I can't get close to people. What if they end up finding me and then I put them in danger? Le . . ." I slam my lips together so I don't blurt out the names of the friends I have made so far.

"Sara . . ." he sighs and then takes a deep breath. "Your friends are safe, and so are you. You can't keep yourself locked in your room all day and night. It isn't normal, sweetheart. They wouldn't want you to live this way. At least promise me that this Christmas you will do more than just lock yourself in your apartment and cry."

Glancing down at my hands, I take a moment to pull my thoughts together. He's right—they wouldn't want me to live this way, but the fear is so close to the surface. I wouldn't know what to do if I put Len, Julia, and Ashley in danger. Not to mention their families. They have been my rocks now for the past seven years. However, I want to make them proud, and I know they're watching from above, probably not happy with the way I've lived the past seven years.

"You're right. I'll see what the girls are doing and go from there. But that's a few weeks away. So, I can't make promises. Thanks for the update on the last deposit," I whisper out.

"You're welcome. You're going to be just fine, Sara. You have my number if you need it. Merry Christmas." With that last parting word, he stands up and walks out of the cafeteria.

I glance around and take another deep breath, seeing that nobody was paying me any attention. Len's going to be coming any second, so I'm grateful that he left when he did. I didn't want to have to explain who he was or what he was doing talking with me.

She invites me to hang with her family every Christmas they're in town. If her brother's stateside or deployed is what determines if they're staying.

"Hey, bitch, what has you in such a deep thought?"

Glancing over, I see Len bouncing her happy self over to me. She's barely two years younger, but you wouldn't ever know it. She's super smart, and I'm grateful we met all that time ago.

"Hey, just trying to figure out what I'm going to do for Christmas. What are your plans this year? Going to visit that sexy brother of yours?" Sexy isn't enough to describe Neil. I haven't met him in person, but from what I've seen in pictures . . . let's just say he has starred in many of my late-night fantasies.

"Okay first, eww. Really, Sara? I told you about calling him sexy to me. He's my brother. I don't view him like that." She takes a deep breath to continue, but I stop her with just one word.

"Dante?"

"Now, he's one sexy piece of man. I just wish he felt the same. I haven't seen him in seven years, and every time I've gone to see Neil, he isn't around. I know he's avoiding me."

"Maybe he's scared and is afraid of what would happen if he's killed and you're left behind? I mean, he writes you religiously, Len. Sorry, but either he just sees you as a baby sister, or he's wanting you but is just afraid. No man puts that kind of commitment into handwriting letters and buying things without thinking one way or the other." I swear that man wants her, but I could be wrong. I haven't met him either. However, the twins tell me their brother wants her which is why I'm leaning more toward that than the other.

"I don't know, Sara, and really don't want to think about it right now." After taking a deep breath, she jumps right back into speaking before I can say a word. "Now, what were we talking about? Oh, Christmas . . . So, this time we are here. Neil's still out on a mission so it's just Mom, Pops, OPG, and me. The De Lucas are going to Italy this year. What are you thinking? Why don't you come and hang with us? You know Pops and Mom would love it, and of course OPG would enjoy seeing the craziness we can cause them."

I take a moment and remember what the detective said and decide that it's time to move on. But that doesn't mean I can let my guard down. Until they're caught, I'm not putting those I've come to love at risk.

"Okay, I would love to join you guys. Do you think your parents truly wouldn't mind?"

"Come on, Sara, you can't sit in your apartment . . . wait . . . what did you say?" I guess I confused her.

"I said okay. But I need to know if your parents would be okay with me joining you. Can you check with them first and let me know?"

"Holy shit! Of course they won't mind. Just so you know, pack a bag. You are joining me in three days when school is done for the holiday. I'm so damn excited! Okay, I'm going to go to my last class. I'm not letting you out of this. Talk soon!" Len jumps up and runs out of the door before I can say one word.

Chuckling to myself, I slowly get up from my seat and grab my bag. I guess I need to get to planning on what I'm packing because I know she isn't going to let me change my mind.

NEIL

God, I just want fifteen minutes to rest before something else comes up. Please, just fifteen minutes.

Today has been a trying day for all of us, and I'm hoping we can get a small break before we're called to do more briefings. The last five months have been hell on all of us, but we knew this was something that could happen. This mission was fucked up, but I'm glad it's done.

"Yo! You packed up and ready to blow this place?" Ghost yells as he walks into the little barrack we are bunking together in.

"Fucking-A, I am. You still heading to Italy to surprise Momma Gio, Poppa Tony, and the twins?" I slowly get off my bunk and stretch out. Since we're finished with the mission early, we got clearance to go ahead and spend the holidays with our families if we wished. Neither of our families has any clue of this, so it will be a great surprise. The only fucking part that sucks is we're only getting one week, and then we have to be back in Cali for debriefing.

"Yep. Flight leaves in about six hours. I'll be there before you set foot in the states. I promise to tell them not to say a word or update Facebook until I know you made it safely. When do you land in Missouri?"

"Tomorrow afternoon. I have Chance picking me up and driving me the back way to your parents' house first. I'll walk over. I want to surprise them, and if they hear a car, I won't get to walk in and see their faces." I walk over to my desk and pack up the few items that I left out for my carry-on. All that's left is taking our bags we want back in Cali to the meet-up space and then we're off to the airport.

"Let's get the fuck out of here. I need a beer while we wait for the damn plane." Ghost picks up his two sea bags, and then his pack for the flight. I do the same and take a moment to look at the place we have stayed at for the past five months. This is one place I'm glad to be leaving. I hope we never come back here. Turning, I walk out the door and get ready to shock the shit out of my family for Christmas.

"Thanks for the ride, Chance. I hope you have a great Christmas with your family. You can keep the change." I hand him a hundred even, though the bill is only forty-two dollars. It's the holidays, and knowing he has a little girl, maybe this will help. I've known Chance since elementary school, and he started his own shuttle business. So anytime we come home to visit, we use him to give us a ride home.

The cold hits me in the face when I step out of the car. Fucking cold sucks. I forgot how freezing the winters are in Kansas City. Plus, we have been in the Middle East, so coming to where the weather is only seventeen degrees with a windchill of eight? Well, let's say my body is saying *fuck you, asshole.*

I take a moment and watch the car drive off, then look toward my parents' house. They aren't home since it's Christmas Eve and after dinner it is tradition that they go to church for the Eve service. This gives me time to get into the house and get settled. I'm excited to see the surprise on their faces at seeing me after being away for five months.

I trudge across the snow and slip into my parents' backyard. Before stepping in through the back door, I spot movement from the window above the garage. I still and watch to see if I spot it again. After five minutes of waiting, I don't see it and just chalk it up to my imagination; I did just get off a nineteen-hour flight.

Stepping inside the back entrance, I turn off the alarm, then reset it after I shut and lock the door. Quietly, I make my way upstairs to my bedroom. The need to drop my bags and take a quick shower before the family get here is overwhelming to say the least. I know I have about three to four hours before they get back. Maybe I can take a nap, too, because they aren't going to let me sleep once they find that I'm home.

I come to a fast stop when I hear murmurs coming from squirt's door. Nobody should be home, and I'm not sure what the hell is going on. I silently put my bag down by my bedroom door, pull out my gun, and make my way to my sister's room. Placing my ear to her door, I listen, trying to make out where the person is. It's then I hear a sound that pulls at my gut, and I realize it's a female giggle.

What in the fuck is going on!

"Ashley, stop and breathe, babe. Len will be back shortly, and we can figure it all out. Okay, maybe not shortly. She told me they would be back around nine and it's only six, so why don't you tell me again what is going on."

"Sara! I can't fucking breathe. What the fuck is wrong with my parents? Why they hell wouldn't they tell me a while ago that I was adopted? I'm not understanding why they would wait until I'm twenty-three to tell me. And on Christmas Eve night!"

I take a moment and realize that Sara must be here to celebrate with my family for Christmas. Normally she isn't with them, even at the urging of my sister every time we celebrated here. Quietly, I walk back to my bag and go into my bedroom. I lock my door and then proceed to unpack.

"Ashley, let's meet for coffee. I'm on my way to the diner down from you. See you soon," I hear from outside my room. Feet stomping down the stairs and out the door makes me run to the window. I see the backside of Sara running to her car. She has long red hair, and it makes something in my chest stir at the sight of it brushing up against her ass. Following the rear lights disappear down the drive, I try to figure out what that stirring was, then decide it isn't worth it. I have to get ready for my family.

The sounds of a car door shutting makes me peek out of the window. A big smile comes across my face to see that my family finally made it home. The lights of another car pulling in causes my family to turn and watch it park. Turning, I rush into the family room and relax back on the couch. I know it might be immature to be excited about surprising my family, but I don't give a shit. I have missed them a lot while I was overseas at the last mission.

"Baby Jesus was just too cute for words. The Scotts were amazing to allow their three-week-old baby to play him. I'm not sure if I would've been that accommodating. He was such a good sport." Moms voice carries through the front door.

"Until he decided two hours was more than enough and decided that Sharon needed to feed him."

"Sara, where did you go?" Squirt pipes up from outside the sitting room.

"I went to see Ashley. She has some stuff going on that I'll explain later."

"Let's go get settled. Time for our opening of presents the Elf left us while we were in church."

I get excited—this is a tradition that my family has done since my first Christmas. It's always brand new PJs and either a new book for each of us or a new family movie for us to watch.

"Elf?" Sara asks as they start to make their way to me.

"Yeah, the Elf comes while we are at church and brings us . . ." is all my sister makes out before I decide it's time to make my presence known.

"Presents to get ready for Santa. But this year he decided to bring something extra." The sound of my voice makes everyone stop and stare at me in shock.

"Neil?" OPG whispers and then rushes me.

"Yeah, it's me. We got finished early, and I decided to surprise my family."

I'm surrounded by the rest of my family within seconds, and it makes me wish I wasn't in the military for a moment. I miss them more than I realize, and I'm beginning to wonder if it's time to call it quits. The movement from my left snaps my eyes that way and that's when I finally get a good look at Sara for the first time. She's beautiful and takes my breath away.

She cocks her head at me and stares like she's trying to figure me out, and then she looks down at her shoes. She starts shaking her head, turns, and walks away. This pisses me off because I want her to stay so I can figure out why I want to grab her, take her upstairs, and bury myself in her for hours. I'm not that type of guy. Yeah, I have fucked a lot of women over the years, but none of them have made me want to pull a caveman on them.

"Hey, where are you going, Sara?" I realize that my voice is fiercer than I intended it to be.

"Hey, be nice to my bestie, Neil." I'm met with a smack against my chest and look down at my sister and cock my eyebrow. She gives me the *what the fuck is wrong with you* look. "Sara's staying with us this Christmas and is a guest. So, don't forget your manners. Now, Sara . . . Where are you going? You need to come and meet this asshole brother of mine, and we have presents to open."

"I was going to go ahead and pack up so I can let you all have time with Neil. I can come back in the morning or tomorrow night. I don't want to take that time away from your family. I know how much you all missed him." Her voice is so quiet I almost don't catch it. Also, the look of sadness on her face makes me want to run to her and demand why.

"No." Her eyes snap at my no, and I see the anger starting to stir in her bright green eyes.

"What do you mean no?" she growls between her clenched teeth.

"You're not going fucking anywhere. *Your ass is here, and that's where it's staying,* is what I mean by no." This not only causes this sexy redhead to gasp out at my demand but also makes the women in my family lose their shit too.

What the fuck is wrong with me?

"Neil, I refuse for you to talk like that to any woman in my house. Say you're sorry right now!" Mom yells.

"Uh, sorry. I don't know what's wrong. What I mean is, there isn't any need for you to leave, okay? Just stay and enjoy the holidays with us. I would like to get to know you better. You're squirt's best friend, and you're always welcome to spend the holidays with us." I finally must have gotten something right because her shoulders drop and then she nods.

Taking a deep breath, I decide the best thing I can do is just ignore her for the rest of the time I'm here. I don't know what it is about her, but something is stirring, and I don't like this shit.

Four

Rebecca

DEAR JOURNAL:

I had another nightmare. This time I was in a crowded place and everyone kept walking by me. I tried to say hello and have conversations with them, and they never responded. They looked right through me. I felt like I was a ghost and that I wasn't even there. Life moved on, and it was like I wasn't ever needed or wanted.

I'm trying to blend in, but I'm wondering if my dream is a prediction on what will happen no matter how much I open up. "He" tells me to open up, make friends, blend in and act normal. But what is "normal?" What does it truly mean to "blend in?" What do they mean to someone like me? Someone who is just a nobody? A number? Alone?

I just want them back . . . I just want what I had

not that long ago . . . I just want to be me, whoever that is. I don't really know anymore . . .

-Rebecca

With a sigh, I sit my book down on the table next to my chair and stare out the window. I really wish I had the answers because at this time . . . I don't know how much longer I can hold on to the hope that this will be over and maybe I can go back to a normal life.

Five

Sara

Present day . . .

I GLANCE BACK IN THE rearview mirror without turning my head. Neil doesn't need to see me looking back at him. That would only give him hope that I was coming back. My breath catches in my throat at the thought of never seeing or hearing his voice again. The pain radiates down my chest, and I wonder if someone could die of heartache.

Thoughts of pain from years ago crowd my mind, and I push it away. This pain is much worse than that time, and I'm struck with the fact that I must love Neil with everything in me, but I can't dwell on that now. I must get home and pack. With what is going on, I know I'll have plenty of time to dissect the feelings that are running deep in my chest right now.

Pulling into my parking spot, I rush into my apartment and grab the suitcase that's buried deep in my closet. It contains everything that is important to me in it. I've always kept it like this because I knew one day I would need it.

The voices from the past start to make it through my mental block, and I start to shake.

"We'll find out who that girl was. It's just a matter of time. The police can't hide her identity forever."

"Which girl?"

"The one from the apartment."

"What are we going to do when we find her?"

I turn my head slightly to see the guys' faces. I didn't see them that night, but I'll never forget the voice that was talking. There isn't much to take in with two of them. I can make out that they're around six feet in height with brown hair and tan skin. But it's the one in the center that makes the hair on my neck rise. He's also around six feet tall with dark brown hair. He looks like he works out a lot, but he has this aura around him that screams control, and that he's in charge. When he raises his head, I see his eyes are like pools of black. They're lifeless almost. The looks on their faces as they whisper what they will do to me, make me shiver and look quickly away. When the bus finally reaches its next station, I rush off, texting the detective. I have to get out of town now that I know they're looking for me. This isn't good.

Squeezing my eyes shut, I will the tears to stop and push the memory to the back of my mind. After a few deep breaths, I grab the two bags that I packed while thinking of the past, along with the handle from the suitcase. As I head to the door, I stop and turn to the bookshelf by the TV. I drop my bags and rush to it. As quickly as I can, I grab the four pictures that I have allowed in my living room. They mean so much to me, and I refuse to leave them behind.

I glance down and see the one of Neil and me from the party for Seal Security. Tears threaten to fall yet again, and I take a moment to gather myself. I don't know how I'm going to get through this, but I can't let my past taint him and his family. It's time to move on. With that thought, I shove the pictures in my bags and hightail it to my car.

I pull up to the police station and sit there looking at the front door. I know Conti is waiting for me, and I'm not sure I want to see him. Since his visit three years ago, I haven't heard from him until the phone call earlier today. The last time I went through this, I left everything behind me, including the family and friends I had made after . . . *No, Sara, don't think of that.*

A few deep breaths later, I'm slowly getting out of my car and starting up the steps. The feeling of being watched has me looking around the parking lot in a panic, wondering if they found me already. My eyes scan everything as I try to get up the steps without being noticed. I glance at the door and see Walters looking out at me with an odd expression.

I know Walters from working at Seal Security, but I got to know him more when Len went missing. He has always given me the creeps, but it started getting worse shortly after Len was found. He's always staring at me like he knows just who I am and knows my story. I know that isn't true—well, he probably knows now, but there was no way before this happened.

"Hey, Sara. What brings you to my domain for once?" he says as he opens the door for me.

"Hi, Detective Walters. I'm here meeting someone."

Walking through, I stop in the lobby area and scan for Conti. When I don't spot him, I pull up my phone to send him a text.

"Who you meeting with? Maybe I can take you to them."

"Detective Vigo Conti. He's here from Florida and has some stuff I need for a case." Lying isn't something I like doing, but if he doesn't know my history, then I don't want to let it out.

Walters cocks his head at me and has a look like he wants to call me out on my shit. I'm hoping he doesn't because I don't want to go into it right now. I don't have time.

"Hmmm, okay. Let me see what I can do. Why don't you come with me and I'll walk you up to the homicide floor where I believe he's at." He takes a step toward me, and something inside me is screaming to tell him to fuck off. Just as I open my mouth to tell him I'll ask the front desk to page him, the side door opens and Conti walks through it, which makes my tension ease.

"Walters. Sara, come with me please." He reaches for my hand and pulls me through the front door, then turns to me. "You okay? You didn't look comfortable talking with Walters."

"He just gives me a bad vibe, is all. But no, I'm not okay, Conti."

Taking a big breath, he nods and then gives me a hug. This causes the tears to come hard.

"It's going to be okay, Sara. We got this, and you're going to be safe. They almost got enough to arrest them. This situation will just be added to the rest, and then they won't be getting out of jail for a long time. Let's get you to safety, okay?"

After pulling myself together, I nod and we head off to wherever the US Marshals decide they need to hide me to keep me safe until this is all done.

I stomp toward my sister's front door, shocked that Sara just drove off without explaining shit. This isn't going to work for me. I need to get my keys and go after her. She isn't getting away from me that easily.

"What the fuck is going on? Why did Sara run off like that?" Sin walks up behind me when I enter the house. I ignore him and head into the kitchen where I proceed to grab my stuff and turn to leave.

"Stop and fucking talk to us, Lucky. We care for her too, and we need to know what the fuck we are going to do to help you figure this shit out." Doc grabs my arm and jerks me to a stop.

I take a deep breath before I knock his ass out. I don't have time to stop and chat as he wants to. My drive to find Sara and get to the bottom of this bullshit is much more important.

"No. I have to fucking go before she disappears. Fucking follow me if you want, but I have to go now." Jerking my arm away from him, I storm out the front door to my bike.

"Neil, listen to reason . . ." Nicoli's voice trails off behind me.

Thoughts of what could be going on run through my

mind. There isn't much we know about Sara other than she's from Alabama and she has no family left. Her parents, who also had no siblings, died in a freak boating accident off the coast of Mexico when they went on an anniversary trip. She was eighteen when this happened, and she moved here to attend school like they wanted her to. Now, with her getting a phone call that freaked her out, I wonder how much of that is bullshit.

The parking lot of her apartment complex comes up in my view, and I quickly scan for her car. Not seeing it anywhere, I take a moment to figure out if I should just drive around or if I should go up to her place. Deciding on the latter, I pull in and start heading up the stairs. The sound of a door shutting behind me has me turning to see that Doc, Sin, Eagle, Carlo, and Nicoli have followed me.

Once I reach her door, I quickly unlock it with a key that I had made a while back. She doesn't know about the key, and I never told her that there were times I would come and watch over her while she slept in the night. That might sound stalkerish to some, but I had to make sure she was okay. She quickly became everything to me three years ago when I got to know her at Christmas. Once I moved back home, I decided that I had to keep a close eye on her. So many times I wanted to go through her things, but I respected her and wanted her to come to me. I needed her to trust me and want to open up to me about what was going on.

"What are we looking for?" Eagle asks as he flips through the mail off to the side of the door.

"Anything that can tell us if she has been here or where she would've gone."

It takes me twenty steps to get to her bedroom door and

for me to realize that she has already been here. The closet door is open, and things are strung out everywhere. Taking a step inside, I quickly start scanning and looking through things left behind. Just when I think I'm not going to find anything, a piece of paper is sticking out of a book. Scanning it raises more questions and now fear that I won't ever be able to find her.

"Find something?" Sin walks into the room, looking at my shaking hands.

"Well, are you going to share or just stand there shaking and make us guess?" Doc ask when I just nod at Sin's question.

I glance up at them at the same time Nicoli and Carlo enter the room, and say what the paper in my hand states. "In case of an emergency, call Detective Conti. Tell him Sara needs him. That she isn't safe anymore."

Six

Sara

PLEASE LET THIS BE A BAD dream.

There's water running somewhere in this small place that I'm attempting to pretend that I'm not in. I'm assuming it's one of the agents in charge of protecting me, but since I haven't gotten out of bed yet to check, well, I'm not sure. I guess maybe it's time to get up and have that talk.

Reaching above my head to stretch, I hit something that's coming from under my pillow. I know immediately what it is, and my heart pulls in my chest. My eyes close as I fight tears that want to rush out—I forgot that I fell asleep holding it under my pillow. It was the only way for me to relax enough to get some sort of sleep. I had to pretend he was with me, holding me, telling me that it will be all right and we would get through it, together.

I slide my hand under the pillow and pull out the object, bringing it up to my face. Gazing at the image, I take a moment to pretend that everything is normal. That we can have a full life together and build the family we both want, or that I think he might want. There was never talk of kids, but seeing him with his nephew leads me to believe a family is what he truly wants. The look of longing on his face reminds me of the night at the cabin. I didn't notice it then, but when I saw this picture after OPG gave it to me, I knew that he did want something more than just a night with me, and that leaving his bed before he woke up that morning was a mistake.

Neil has his arms wrapped around me from behind and is looking down at me. I'm looking over at Andy and Chris, laughing at something they said. I look so carefree and happy, but that isn't what has my attention when I look upon this image. It isn't the way his hands wrap around my waist, or the look of pure longing and desire that is clearly showing in his expression. It isn't the look of wonder as he gazes at my face that's on his shoulder from the laughter that I couldn't contain. It isn't lust that's shining in those deep, blue-green eyes. No, it's the deep, uncontrollable, undying love that's shining so bright.

Something that I missed when I looked at him before.

I knew he kept it hidden from me when I looked at him, but what I couldn't understand is why. What could possibly stop him from telling me or at least showing me the feelings that he truly had for me? Because if I'm honest with myself, I share those same deep emotions with him. The feelings that run within me don't even compare to what I felt . . . and the thought that comes next is why I can't have him. Why I never expressed just how much he meant to me. How much he was my real reason for taking each breath that is needed to live, and the reason why I'm protecting him from my past.

"Sara, you awake?" The knock and voice at my door has me shoving the picture back under my pillow and swallowing back the burning sensation from the back of my throat.

As I wipe the tears from my face, I clear my throat and answer out, "Yeah, just give me a moment, please."

"Okay, take your time. Detective Conti will be here with breakfast shortly, and we need to go over the plans."

"Sounds good."

Getting out of bed, I start to get ready for the day. Let's hope that we can find a better place for me to hide, because I think the next time they find me, I'll end up dead.

"Breakfast okay?" Detective Winters ask as she gets me more coffee.

"Yes. Thank you for everything you guys have done for me. I'm not sure what to do next. How the hell did they find me? I thought we were safe since only two of you knew where and who I really am. How many more now know?" Detective Winters takes a deep breath, and then she takes a seat next to Conti.

"Someone got your file. We aren't sure if it was from Conti's office or from my office. There's an investigation happening to find out where the information was leaked from, but trust us when we say it isn't something that happens often. Right now, we're just going to hang out here at the safe house. There's only one other detective that knows where we are and what has happened. He's trusted and will be a part of your protection detail," Winters explains, then looks over at Conti.

"Where are we, exactly?"

"The less you know the better, Sara. It might be a while, is there anything you need or want us to get for you? Winters is heading back and will bring back everything you need."

"Not right now. I think I have everything. If I think of something, I'll write it down so then we can get it next round, if that's okay. But I do have a question. What did you tell Neil?" My throat closes a bit on his name and makes me swallow hard to prevent tears from forming again.

"Nothing yet. I know he came to the station looking for me. He found a paper that had my name on it. Something about it being stuck in a book by your bed." His eyebrow arches at me.

Shit!

"Not the smartest thing to do there, Sara. Next time don't do that. Trust me. Our files are flagged anytime your name is put through the system, so we would've known something is up," Winters scolds me as she reaches for her notes to leave.

"I'm sorry—I just wanted to make sure I was covered if I went missing. I won't do that again. What are you going to tell him? I'm worried about my friends too and what they're going to do."

"Not sure yet, but I have a bit of time to come up with something. I'm here for the next three days. Let's work it out together." Conti stands and walks Winters to the door.

Needing a moment to myself to get through the feelings plaguing me, I head to my room and shut the door behind me, hoping Conti gets the point that I need a minute. When I reach my bed, I reach under the pillow and pull out the picture again. Tears start as the thought of never seeing my friends and Neil again rolls through my body.

"I love you, Neil. I'm sorry I will never get to express it to you in person. I just hope you know that you mean more than anything to me, even if that means I'll never see you again," I whisper to the image in my hand before I lay down and cry as quietly as I can into my pillow.

NEIL

It's been three days since I've heard from Sara or the detective. I've called the number the station gave me daily and left messages for him to call me back with answers. We've poured over all the files we have and could find at the office. Still—nothing. It's beginning to piss me off.

The research and digging I did on Detective Vigo Conti didn't tell me much. He's from Pensacola Florida and has a sister, Madison, who he has custody of. She has autism and needs around-the-clock care. Currently, a private nurse is taking care of her while he's here in Missouri. He works for the Special Victim and Homicide unit in the Pensacola Police Department—PPD. I also saw he worked with US Marshals as well, which now makes me wonder if Sara is in something much more than I thought she could be involved in.

"Why would she be involved with Conti? What are your thoughts on that and why she would need him contacted?" Ghost murmurs. He and the twins are going through the paperwork on Conti, trying to see if he can spot anything that I might have missed.

"Fuck if I know. I don't see her being part of a crime. The only thing I can think is that she witnessed a crime and now she's part of Witness Protection. If that's the case, then we aren't going to get anything out of this paperwork. Their cases are always closed tight, and there's no getting them open. But what type of crime did she see that would need this level of protection?" I have no clue why I asked that because there isn't going to be an answer that I'm willing to accept. Any crime my Sara saw isn't going to be one I'm okay with her witnessing.

"It would've had to involve death since he's a homicide . . ." My phone rings, cutting off Doc. I glance down and see it's the fucking detective, finally.

"Shields."

"Hello, Mr. Shields, I just got back into town and received your messages. Is there somewhere we can meet to talk?" It's the detective finally calling me back.

"I'm at my office—why not just swing by?" I offer, hoping he takes what I'm giving him because I want my guys around when we "talk."

"Be there in fifteen." Then the line goes dead.

"Get shit ready. He will be here shortly. Let's do this in the conference room. I'll wait in my office."

Walking into my office, I head straight for my desk and take a seat. I just need a few moments to get my shit together and hope like hell I can handle whatever shit storm this detective is going to try to throw my way.

After a few moments, I turn toward my computer and bring it back to life. The image that pops up takes my breath away as I stare at it. She looks breathtaking and the expression on her face tells me more than she ever let on. I think back to when the image was taken, and I'm grateful that OPG could capture it.

I'm standing off to the side of her with my arm thrown around her shoulder. I was talking to Sin, and she was staring up at my face. The image shows the true feelings that she never conveyed to me. They show me that I'm not alone in my feelings for her. Her face is soft, and her eyes are staring intently at me. They're fully open, and not hiding anything. There's a mix of pure love and longing. They show just how much she wants to be with me, however there's also a mix of sadness that I hadn't noticed before. Now that she's gone, I'm wondering if that's why.

The knock on my door has me shaking off the thoughts clouding my brain.

"Yeah."

"He just pulled up."

Nodding, I quickly sign into my computer and then turn on the camera in the conference room so we can go over the video later after he leaves to see if there's something we can catch on to. After making sure the sound and video are recording, I head into the conference room to get answers. What Conti doesn't know is he isn't leaving until we know what's going on, because I'm not letting Sara get away this time.

"Conti, what the fuck is going on, and where the fuck is Sara?" Doc spouts as I walk in.

"I'll explain what I can and what I'm allowed to say." Conti gives me a look that says not to argue, but he hasn't seen just how fucked up I can get when I want answers. I can feel the rage starting to flood my veins at what he could be hiding.

"Shit. Lucky, we need answers before you attempt to kill him, plus how much good will you be for Sara if you're in jail for killing the detective?" Sin's voice slowly enters my brain.

"What do you mean, you will tell us what you can? Do you understand who we are and that we care for Sara? Do you get that she's safe with us and that we would do anything to protect her? Do you also understand that she's my fucking *life*?" By this point I'm in his face. I don't give a shit if I get in trouble—this prick isn't leaving until I'm satisfied with what I'm told.

"Neil, that's enough. Sit down now so we can get answers." Ghost pulls me away and shoves me in a chair next to him.

"Are you done?" Conti questions, as he looks me straight in the eye.

Ballsy asshole.

After a few deep breaths, I just give him a nod because if I open my mouth, I'm going to go off again.

"Now, why don't we cut the bullshit. What do you know?" His question makes Sin chuckle and shake his head.

"We know who you are, who you work for, your family members, and that you're here to help Sara, but that's about all we got." Eagle cracks his head after he spouts out the short answer.

"I figured you checked into things during these past few days." He looks over toward me and arches his brow before he continues. "What I can tell you is that she's safe and that she will be in contact when she can. She asked me to give you this package that I brought with me. That said, what I will pass on is that more than likely you won't see her again, and won't have contact with her. After today, you won't see me again and before you make threats against me, know that it isn't that I don't want to tell you, it's that my hands are tied against telling you and that I am bound by law."

"What. In. The. Ever. Loving. Fuck do you mean we won't see or hear from her or you? I swear to God, Detective, I won't hold him back if you don't start talking!" Ghost slams his hands on the table in front of him. Nicoli places a hand on his shoulder, trying to calm him.

Rage is pouring off of me right now, and I clench the arms of the chair even tighter trying to hold off from beating this piece of shit in front of me.

"Guys, just give him a chance to speak, will you?" Carlo stands and walks over to the coffee station.

"Look, I want to tell you everything, but I can't. The package will explain more. Just, please, for her safety, don't look deeper and don't try to find her." With that, he puts the package down and walks out the door without looking back.

I stare at the package in front of me, and I'm not sure if I want to open it. I'm not sure if I want to accept that I won't see her again. Ever so slowly, I get up from my chair and reach out for the package. Opening the top, I look down and see two things: a stack of letters and a picture that's of her and me.

It sinks in that she's trying to end things between us before they fully started. She's attempting to protect me and those around me. Shaking my head, I close the box and walk away from it because I'm not ready to accept defeat . . . not yet.

Seven

Rebecca

DEAR JOURNAL:

It has been six months since I wrote in this damn thing. I have been seeing someone who helps me with the nightmares. I also made a few friends here in this new place. I still think that I don't belong. That I'm a nobody now. I feel like a fraud. I feel like that because I can't tell them who I really am. I fell and hurt my ankle, which led to a trip to the doctor. I was prescribed pain pills . . . which numb more than just my hurt ankle.

I got another script today. I'm hoping it continues to numb me. Maybe they will help me find out who I really am supposed to be. Maybe, I'll finally feel normal and blend in more.

-Rebecca

I put my pen down on top of my journal and place my head in my hands. God, what am I really going to do? Glancing over at my table, I see the bottle just sitting there, calling to me to open it and just take one. I take a moment and think if I really should just end my life. Would they miss me? Would anyone even know? How long would it take for someone to recognize I wasn't there anymore?

"Hey, you there, woman? Let's go get coffee!" a voice from the hall of my apartment pulls me from my thoughts. It's one of the new friends I made. Coffee does sound good. I look back over and take two pills from the bottle. Tossing them back with a gulp of water, I turn to the door, and swing it open with a fake smile on my face.

"Yep, let's go!" I turn and lock my door quickly before heading out. I just hope the pills kick in fast.

Eight

Sara

IT'S BEEN A WEEK SINCE I had to leave my life behind. A week of wondering what Neil's doing. A week of wondering if Len is getting bigger. A week of wondering if I'm safe enough to be moved yet. Thoughts of the last time this happened rushes through my mind, and I'm scared that this time I won't make it to safety.

"Sara, you busy?" Winters ask through my door.

"Come in."

Winters walks in and looks around the room before she takes a seat on the chair by my closet. "How you holding up?"

Taking a moment, I think about how I feel and what has happened. Since I've been here, I've only seen Conti once and that was three days ago. He's due back tomorrow, and I'm eager to find out what happened with Neil. We decided to just explain that I'm safe, and that I wouldn't be seeing him again. I wrote all of them notes telling them how much they meant to me, and that if things changed—maybe one day I can come back.

"Sara?"

"Sorry, I'm thinking of what the next move is going to be. Conti is due back tomorrow and then we'll go over more, right?"

"That's what he explained to me on the phone. He said he got more information for us, and he talked with Neil. I just wanted to check in on you. Do you need anything before he gets here?"

Tears fill my eyes at the sound of Neil's name, and I quickly shake my head and look down at my lap hoping she will leave the room to let me cry in peace. Unfortunately, I'm not that lucky because I feel the bed move from her sitting next to me, and she wraps her arms around my shoulders.

"Sara I'm sorry this is happening. We're trying everything to find where the leak is and to finish this off so hopefully you can get back to the life that you have created there."

"I don't think I'll ever get to come back, and I don't think they will ever trust me again. I didn't tell them everything about me, and I lied about my life. You have to understand; I know Neil, and he can't stand liars. Even though I have a good reason to keep it from him—I know he won't ever trust me again." The sobs I try to hold back come out full force.

"I have a feeling you're wrong, sweetheart. That man was calling Conti multiple times a day to get answers. Someone like that wouldn't just drop you. Let's focus on getting this case closed tight so you can go back, okay?"

I nod just to get her to leave me be, because she doesn't understand what I wrote in the letter. None of them do, and I know the words that I said in it will be what really kills any chance I have with Neil and will be what really ends any hope I have of being with him in the future.

I hear murmurs coming from the other room, and it takes me a moment to open my eyes.

Ugh, I feel like I have been running sandpaper on my inner lids.

Rubbing them, I remember that I cried myself to sleep while Winters held me. That makes me wince at what she must think of me. I check the clock really quick and see that it's four in the morning. I slept the whole afternoon and night away. The other voice I hear must be Conti, which means I need to get up and get some coffee in me so we can get things hashed out and going.

Slowly, I get off the bed and change my clothes. I really want a shower, but I think I'll do that after the talk. After I quickly throw on a pair of sweats and T-shirt, I rush over to the dresser to brush my hair. I wince at the sight I see in the mirror.

My hair is a rat's nest, my face is pale from the amount of time I have been in the safe house, and my eyes are swollen from the crying mess I was yesterday. My lips looked cracked, and it looks like I've also lost weight because my once-fitting shirt is slightly big on my frame.

Thank God Neil can't see me right now because this would be a total turnoff, and I'm not sure I can take that look in his eyes.

Damn it, Sara, stop thinking about him. You told

yourself no more thoughts of him as you fell asleep crying last night.

After a few deep breaths, I hurriedly get things done so I can go and face the detectives. The murmurs get louder as I round the corner, and I come to a stop when I see it's just Winters and she's leaning against the counter on the phone. Cocking my head, I look around her hoping to spot Conti on the other side possibly.

"Winters, I need to know where you're at, damn it. We're supposed to finish this case, and I can't do that without you. So, just tell me where you're at, and I'll bring by the paperwork." I suck in a deep breath at the voice on the other line. Winters turns her head to me and shakes it while holding her finger up to her mouth letting me know to stay silent.

"Sin, I'll be in town later today and I'll meet you at Seal Security. I need to get off of here, so I'll call when I'm ten minutes out." She hangs up on Sin before anything else can be said.

"Does he know?"

"No. Nobody knows that I'm here with you. Now, coffee?" I nod at her question and walk over to the fridge to get stuff out to make breakfast. It's the least I can do since she let me cry on her shoulder last night. Speaking of which . . .

"Look, Winters, about last night . . ."

"Sara, stop. I know you're a strong, independent woman and you don't like to be viewed as weak. Everyone has a breaking point," she states, then turns, pours my coffee, hands it to me, and then walks away.

Well, I guess that ends that. My stomach lets me know

that I didn't eat last night so I start on breakfast while waiting for Conti to get here.

Five hours later, after we have eaten breakfast and drank more coffee than most humans really should consume, Conti finally shows up and brings what I need. However, he couldn't find the item I'm still searching for. I think for a brief moment that it might be at work. But I'm not one hundred percent sure. The thought of work has me thinking about Conti seeing Neil. I'm not wanting to ask, but I need to know what happened when he saw him before we start figuring out what we are going to do now.

"Conti. Um . . . How did it go?" I realize my voice is barely a whisper.

"He was upset and demanded to know what was going on. I gave him the box you asked me to and left. I haven't heard from him since."

I absorb his words for a moment, then nod and stand up. This is what I wanted, right? No matter that the answer to that question is a yes, it still makes my heart hurt hearing that he didn't demand more answers, or contact him for information. Even if he did, I know Conti wouldn't have said anything, and if Neil tried to call my phone, it wouldn't have mattered because it has been turned off.

"Sara . . ." The raise of my hand cuts Winters's voice off from whatever she was going to say.

"I just need a few moments, please." Walking into my room, I go straight to my book and open it up to the last page.

God does give you things you can't handle. However, He won't give you things that He can't handle. So, lean on him and let him carry the burdens that aren't yours to carry.

Momma's voice is what I hear when I read these words, and I feel my tears fall as my throat tightens at the thought that I'm physically alone because at times like this I don't feel God is real or with me.

NEIL

I take a look around my office and wonder for the millionth time if I am ever going to find Sara and get to the bottom of what is going on. The thought of her has me glancing at my bookcase again.

Fucking Detective Conti and his, "Don't look for her," command.

Something brown catches my eye, which makes me remember that I haven't read the letter that she wrote me yet.

Fuck it.

Standing up, I walk over to grab the box that he left. I don't think I'm ready to read it, but at this point in our search, I'm at a loss. I'm hoping that this will help us find her. The walk back to my chair seems to take forever because of the dread that's sinking inside my stomach. The only thing left in the box is the letter and pictures of both of us that she had.

They're from that night at the lake, and it makes me smirk thinking of what we shared. The images also show me just what I had been missing all this time–she's in love with me like I am with her.

The thoughts of that night rush back to me . . .

"What's up, brother?" Ghost questions, which makes me sigh out at the thought that he caught me watching Sara again.

"I don't know what to do with Sara." I glance back over at her. "I want her to open up to me, and now that Len is here, I figured she would, but she isn't talking. I want to run a background check on her, but I have a feeling she will know that I did it."

"What do you think it is?" He cocks his head at the question.

"No fucking clue, but I know it's bad," I state, feeling angry at the thought that she's hiding something from me.

I turn back to Sara and see that she's relaxed, but there's a haunted gaze in her eyes that has been there since I met her three years ago. I've always wondered what put it there, but I know from Len that she never talks to anyone about her past. My heart starts to ache at the thought that my beautiful girl has seen something that makes her have fear that pours from her body and eyes.

"What if you get her drunk and then kind of do an interrogation on her?" Ghost says with humor lacing his voice. We both know that isn't going to work.

"Hmmm . . . that could work, or it could backfire. Maybe once all this shit with Adams is done, I can talk with Len and we can figure out a way to get her to let us in. I'm tired of waiting for her—three years of this is long enough," I murmur as I stand up and start heading over to her. It's time that I at least show her what it will be like to be mine.

I make it to her in less than thirty steps and catch her eye. Her face slowly transforms at the sight of me. Bending down, I whisper, "Let's go, Habibti."

She glares at me, shakes her head, and crosses her arms in a defiant pose. What she doesn't realize is that she isn't going to have a choice. I'm done waiting. Fuck this shit. Smirk in place, I bend down quickly, throw her over my shoulder, and turn toward the house.

"Fucking put me down, Neil! I don't want to talk." She's hitting my back, but it doesn't slow my pace. A body blocks my path, and anger fills me when I see it's Sin. He knows how I feel about her, so why is he stopping me? I'm not sure, but this is fucked up, and I refuse to allow him to take her from me. I guess the look on my face doesn't deter him because he steps behind me. I wish I could see her face, but the fear of putting her down and her getting away is too strong.

"Sara, if you want to be put down I'll make it happen, but, sweetheart, I think you really need to speak with him in private. He isn't going to hurt you or do anything you don't want him to do. But the choice is yours. Do you want me to make him put you down?" Rage flows through me at the thought that Sin would do just what he said. I also know he would get Doc and Eagle to help, and honestly, I wouldn't keep her if she truly didn't want to talk to me. Saying a quick prayer, I hold my breath at her answer.

"No," she whispers so quietly that I almost don't hear it. Sin takes a small step back, and smirks at me, nodding his head. Damn, this girl is going to be the death of me. After a slap to her ass for fighting me, I rush her into my room. Quickly, I shut the door and then walk her over to the bed and toss her onto it. She's so tiny compared to me.

"Neil, what are you doing? Why did you bring me in

here?"

"Habibti, enough is enough. We both . . ."

"What does that mean? I've heard you call me it a few times, but I have no clue what it truly means."

Shit, I keep forgetting I haven't told her what it means. "It's a term of endearment in Arabic. It's what a man calls the woman he loves. The year after I met you, I went to Iraq and overheard a man say it to his wife, and it reminded me of you." I watch as her face softens at the explanation.

Seeing her relax at those words makes me hard, and I can't hold back anymore. I rush over to her and push her down onto her back as I take her lips in a hard kiss. She arches her back and wraps her arms around my neck while moaning loudly at the contact of our lips.

I tear my lips from hers and grind my cock against her pussy, which causes her to moan even louder. I hear footsteps rushing out in the hall and look down at her flushed face.

"If you don't stop those noises, I'm going to gag you, Sara," I growl at her because, damn it, nobody should be able to hear the pleasure that comes out of her lips when she's turned on. I see a spark of interest at the thought of being gagged in Sara's eyes. Interesting. What she doesn't know is that I'm not into hardcore BDSM, but I am very dominant in bed. This is something we can explore. I know she's a submissive, but she's also very fiercely independent.

I hear laughing and realize it's Ghost and Len. Damn it, I really don't need my sister to hear what I'm doing. For a brief moment, I feel Sara stiffen at the sound, and I want to scream because I know she's going to want to stop now. The feeling of shaking catches me off guard and has me *glancing down again at her face. The sound of laughter burst from her lips, making me chuckle.*

"Fuck, Sara, I thought that would scare you off."

"Oh, my God. Neil, I'm never going to be able to face them tomorrow." Her chuckles start to get louder.

"I can find something to gag you with if you don't stop," I warn again with a smirk, which causes her to stop at that moment. "You like the idea of me gagging you, Habibti?"

"Yes."

"Good to know. Now, where were we?"

The knock at the door pulls me out of my thoughts and has me tossing the box on the desk.

"Hey, Coleman is on line two and needs to talk to you." Ghost strolls in and plops in the chair in front of me.

The thought of what he might need has my raging hard-on deflating in my pants.

"What's up, Coleman?" I ask, putting the phone on speaker, grabbing my notebook and pen so I can take notes. I need to also see if Coleman and his crew would be willing to help me look for Sara. But first, I really need to read the note she left me and talk to the girls about their notes.

"I need a solid. I need you to find someone for me," he grunts.

"Hit me with it," I state and then start writing down what he's telling me.

After hanging up with Coleman, I turn to Ghost. "Let's get this over with quickly. I need to get back to finding Sara."

Nine

NEIL

***

"SHIT. COLEMAN ISN'T GOING TO like this," Sin says off to the right of me. I just nod because he's right. Pulling out my phone, I place the call that isn't going to be pleasant to deliver.

"Yo!"

"Yo? What the fuck? That's not how you answer the phone professionally. What's going on?" I ask him because he sounds breathless.

"Nothing much, just finished PT. What can I do you for, man?"

"That present you gave us? Well, we got some information that you'll want, if you got a second?" I'm holding my breath because part of me wants him to say that he's busy.

"Tell me," he growls.

Shit.

Taking a deep breath, I continue. "What does the name

Morrison mean to you? From what this fuckhead told us, he's an ex-employee, and he has a major grudge against the Townsends."

"I'll have to ask Brett about him—the name doesn't sound familiar. What is he planning?"

"The only thing he could tell us is that this Morrison called him a couple of times offering him money due to the debts this dipshit racked up in gambling. His job was to open the door and let some guy into the house at a certain time and day. By doing that, he would be debt free," I growl the last bit and stare at the fuckhead that's still tied to the chair.

Ghost grabs the phone from me and places it on speaker. "Hey, Coleman, there's more. We need to find this Morrison guy. I guess he has a major issue with the Townsends. This piece of shit said that he couldn't wait until the Townsends get what's coming to them. That it's about time they were brought down. It doesn't look good, man, and I'm worried things are going to get bad for you all."

"What if I send Sin to help find this Morrison?" I shout, looking over at Sin to make sure he's cool with it.

"Yeah, find the piece of shit and give him to the Feds. I want this done officially, and made public, so that whoever is heading this knows that we're closing in on him," Coleman directs us.

"And what do you want me to do with this piece of fucking trash I have in my custody?"

"Keep him. I'll send someone to collect him and bring him back to Piersville. He's the only one who can identify this fucker who cut the step, and I want that asshole!" he seethes.

"Sin, can bring the piece of shit to you since he's on his

way to help find Morrison. Talk soon." I hang up after he says his thanks.

"Let's get this shit over with. Sin, take him to Piersville and help Coleman find this Morrison fuck. Ghost, I need you with me at the office."

We help Sin get fuckhead in the car, and then we head off to the office. Now that that's finished, it's time to find my girl.

The conference room table is filled with pictures and paperwork, which is driving me up a wall. I like order, and it just seems like since Sara left it has been nothing but chaos.

"Did you read the letter yet?" Ghost asks as he shuffles through yet another stack of papers.

"Nope."

"What the fuck, Lucky? Read it already. It might hold a key for us to find her," Doc pipes up from behind me.

I know they're right, but I don't want to read it yet. I have a feeling it's a fucking "Dear John" letter, and if that's what it is, then it will end up pissing me off even more.

"I'm going to go look at the filing cabinet again." I storm out of the room because I'm not ready to talk to them about this shit.

The filing cabinet that Sara uses is off to the right of her desk. She keeps our files together for us, and I know she has her own "drawer" she uses to store shit in but none of us really go through it. Right as I reach the cabinet, I see something sparkling off to the side. Bending over, I spot a heart necklace, which I quickly pick up.

Someone must have dropped it.

It happens so often—just last week we found a bracelet, and we have no clue who it belongs to. I feel something on the other side of the heart which has me turning it over and holding it up to my face to read it.

S, I'll always be with you. Love, R.

Shit. I wonder if this is Sara's, and if it is, then who the fuck is R? I swear if it's someone from her past . . . damn it, Neil, keep your fucking head. You don't even know if this is hers!

After a few deep breaths, I turn back to the task at hand. I feel like I'm violating her space by digging through her drawer, but I need answers. There really isn't much in here: shit for her period, a small bag of makeup, hair products, some candy, a small box that has tons of random stuff in it, and a few bottles of Diet Coke. I take in the box again and spot a note taped to it that says, "L&F," which I figure out quickly means "Lost and Found." I place the necklace in there just in case it isn't Sara's.

Just as I'm getting ready to close the drawer, I spot a notebook journal in the box. On the front, there's a stenciled script that says, "Remembering Rebecca."

That's odd . . . Why would someone leave this behind?

I look through the journal, and the handwriting is familiar but different. I don't want to read someone's personal writings, but I'm curious to see who this is.

Tucking the notebook under my arm, I quickly shut the drawer and then head to my office to do some reading. It's the distraction I need from opening that damn letter Sara left me.

Sara

Shit, where is it? It has to be here . . . there's no way I lost it!

I'm trying not to lose my mind because I can't find it anywhere. I know I didn't take it out often—well, I did take it out when I needed to remember and needed that connection, but I don't remember ever not putting it back.

"Sara, you okay?"

Looking to my right, I see Winters looking at me with concern shining bright in her eyes.

"Yeah, why do you ask?"

"You're clutching at your neck and have a look of panic across your face. Are you having an allergy attack or having problems breathing?"

It takes me a second to realize that my hand is at my neck, right where a necklace would be, and I quickly drop my hand.

"I'm just searching for something I think I might have forgotten. I'll keep looking, and if I can't find it, I might need you or Conti to look for it at my apartment. Everything okay with you?"

"Yep. I just thought I would let you know lunch is ready. Why don't you come eat, and maybe it will help you think of the last place you had whatever it is you're missing." Winters turns and walks out my door.

I really hope she's right.

After lunch, I ended up searching my room another fifteen times at least. I have concluded that I must have misplaced it. I explained to Winters what I'm looking for, and she said she would contact Conti to look in my apartment. I know it sounds stupid and it's just a little thing, but they really need to understand how important it is to me to have this item.

"Sara, I need you in here a second. Conti just called and he has some news."

Shit, I hope it's good and that it means maybe I can finally get my life back again.

It takes me a moment to make it into the living room, and I spot her at the couch but she has a huge stack of papers in front of her on the table. She's such a beautiful woman, and I wonder if she has a love at home waiting for her.

"Winters, tell me about yourself. I know I probably should have asked this before, but you are so beautiful, and I really hope I'm not keeping you from someone."

Her blue eyes connect with mine, and I can see the slight redness creep up on her cheeks. She's about my height and can't weigh any more than one-thirty. She has beautiful curly brown hair and these chic glasses that fit her face, and olive-toned skin that has a soft glow about it.

"Umm, no, I'm not with anyone. I did have a boyfriend, but he said I was too controlling and didn't like the fact that I was a detective," she murmurs, and I smile at the thought of her standing up to him with her job.

"Good—I'm glad you stood your ground."

"I did, but I need a guy who isn't going to take my shit at home. I'm tired, and when I get home, I don't want to take charge. I want to just sit back, but it isn't in my nature to give up and not do something that needs to be done. Honestly, I don't know how to relax and let someone take the reins. I need someone who will do that with me." The look on her face shows that she's really wanting someone to take care of her, and love her for her, but take charge when need be. It reminds me of how Neil is that way. My heart aches at the thought of him, and I push it away again.

"I get it. I wish things were different and we could be friends. I think you would get along with the girls . . ." I trail off because tears start to surface again.

"Me too," she softly murmurs, and then looks down at the papers again. "Okay, come sit. We got some intel, and Conti needs you to know there's a new detective coming. He's going to take his place in helping guard you. He hasn't told me who it is, but he has to go back to Florida for a brief moment to meet up with some people, and to check on his sister."

"New detective? Winters, is this going to be the break we need? Am I going to be able to go back to my life?" I ask as I take a seat next to her.

"It just might be, but we aren't sure. Now, here's what we know . . ."

Ten

Rebecca

DEAR JOURNAL:

I almost ended it the other day. What stopped me? I saw an image of the most beautiful man alive, and it made me stop and second-guess everything. The feelings he brought out in me I thought I would never feel again. I thought they were dead. I thought they would be forever buried with Arturo. However, I realized the love I thought I had for Arturo . . . just might not have been love after all. The feelings this guy brings out, I'm not sure what they are, really. Can it be love? Or is it just major lust? I mean, it was just a picture for God's sake! But it made me dump the pills down the toilet and second guess if I might be able to have that normal life. Maybe, just maybe, I'm not a ghost or a number . . . maybe I am finally figuring out who I truly am.

One day I'll meet him, but until that day . . . I just need to continue to find out who and what I am going to do with myself.

-Rebecca

I toss the book and pen on the table and turn back to the window to my left. I'm not sure what to think of these feelings, but I'm wondering if God is finally going to give me what I truly want. I'm hoping so, because I have to do some things soon that I'm not looking forward to. Maybe having the guy from the picture, that's now imbedded into my head, to dream and think about will help me get through the next week of what I feel is going to be hell.

Eleven

NEIL

***

"LUCKY, WE NEED TO CALL the boys and see if they can help. Now that the twins are in Italy for a few months, I suggest we give Mace a call. He has a way with getting info we don't know how to find," Ghost suggests as he's getting coffee for us both.

"Sounds good." I reach over, hit speaker, and dial up Mace.

Answering in his normal brusque manner, Mace clipped, "Masias."

"Mace, got a moment? There's something special that I need help on."

"Shields? Sure, what's up? Y'all okay?" He sounded genuinely concerned.

"Fuck, Mace. It's a cluster fuck. Has Sin filled you in on what's going on over here? I know he's been in your area for a few weeks now, but I'm not sure if he's had a chance to tell you everything. I also don't know if you are in town or out." I'm really wondering if I should call Coleman because I know they have a lot going on with the shit that they're going through too.

"Don't worry, man. My sister's here, so I'm holed up at home for a bit. Sin mentioned some shit, but didn't really go into big details. Tell me what you need done."

I look over at Ghost and he nods, letting me know that I just need to reach out and ask for help. As much as it guts me, I know it's the best thing that needs to happen. I'm too close to this case, so to speak, and I know fresh eyes will help find out what I can't seem to. After briefly filling him in on what's going down, I take a deep breath and go for it.

"I need some help on finding out what Sara's hiding, man. Something happened, and right now the only thing we know is that she's in hiding and that she's being protected by these detectives. Also, if you can find where she is right now, that would help. It's like she dropped off the planet."

"Send me the names of the detectives and all of the details you have on her. Name, DOB, and shit like that. Once we get that in the system, we'll know what we're dealing with. I'll get Harvey to use the spook system so that the search for her doesn't show up. You never know who's fucking watching, right?"

The thought that someone is watching her files pisses me off more than I can even express. Ghost sees the anger coming over me and walks over, snatching the phone off the cradle.

"We'll get the stuff to you. If you think of anything else you want or need, just message me. Anything we can help you with while you're doing this?" Ghost says. I can't hear what's said from there, but I take a moment to pull my thoughts together. After a few moments, I grab the phone back from Ghost.

"Mace, thanks, man. I owe you."

"Fuck that, Shields; brothers for life, yeah? I'll let you know ASA-fuckin-P what I find out. I'll get Harvey to make it a priority."

"Brothers for life. Talk to you soon." I hang up the phone and look over at Ghost. This is going to be the longest wait of my life.

Sara

After Winters and I had our talk, I decided that I needed to take a hot bath and soak for a while. I'm not looking forward to meeting a new detective, but I have to trust that they know what they're doing.

Leaning back in the bubbles with my eyes closed, thoughts of Neil and myself rush to the front of my mind. I think about stopping them, but the music that's playing softly adds to the moment. This will be okay, right? Allowing the thoughts in the bathroom where I can cry if needed? *Black* by Dierks Bentley starts playing, and it takes me back to that one night that my world went black by his touch . . .

After the scene downstairs and hearing everyone laugh at Neil's antics at wanting to get me alone, I can feel the red creep up on my cheeks. I'm glad the room is somewhat dark and he can't see the blush that's moving up my body. It also doesn't help that Len and Dante heard my moans and Neil's comment about gagging me. However, the thought of him taking control and doing dirty things has me getting even wetter between my thighs.

The movement above me has me looking through my eyelashes at the man that owns my heart. The thought that my past can hurt him has me thinking twice about continuing anything with him. Maybe I should stop this now.

"Now, where were we?"

"Neil, I think we should . . ." His hand covers my mouth before I can get another word in.

"Habibti, just give me tonight to show you a tiny part of what it would mean to be mine. I can't keep playing these cat-and-mouse games with my feelings. Please, just give me tonight, and in the morning, we'll talk, yeah?" His eyes are pleading for me to agree with him.

Can I just give him tonight? Will I be able to walk away after this night? Because I can't put him in danger. The voice in the back of my head tells me to trust him and do it, but there still is the lingering doubt. Still staring into his beautiful blue-green eyes, I see that he's struggling to hold on to his control and he's begging for me to say yes. I see the moment when he thinks I'm going to demand him to leave me be, and the pain in my heart at the hurt that's starting to show has me softly nodding my acceptance. Shock fills his eyes as they go wide at my movement.

"You won't regret this, Sara." Moving his hand, he takes my lips with his own and gives me a soft, yet very possessive kiss.

His hands remove my clothing. He pulls back just enough so he can rip my tank off me, and then goes right *back to kissing me. Within minutes, he has me bare before him.*

He starts slowly kissing down my neck, making his way down my chest and over to my right nipple. He glances up at me with a smirk as he takes my peak into his mouth. This causes me to let out a loud moan and arch my back to him. Suddenly, he's off my body and standing before me.

"I told you, Habibti, I would gag you if you made a sound." He reaches down and pulls up the thong I was wearing, and he also grabs my tank. "If at any moment you aren't okay with what I'm about ready to do, I want you to knock twice on the headboard. Understand?" With a nod from me, he quickly wraps the thong around my hands and ties them to the headboard, then takes the tank and starts to wrap it around my eyes.

"Neil . . ."

"Trust me, Sara." He stares at me and gives me a moment to think about it. Finally, I nod, and he covers my eyes. I feel him get off the bed, then hear noise around the room. Then, I feel his hand on my face. "Open your mouth, Habibti." I slowly open, and he places something soft between my lips, then wraps it around my head.

"Fuck me. You look amazing laid out for me. Now, where was I?" He goes back to kissing down my chest until he reaches my nipple. "I want you to let your mind go. Just concentrate on my touch."

I feel his warm tongue touch my nipple. The softness of his lips closes around it as he sucks it into his mouth. Jesus, it feels amazing. I haven't had a man's touch like this since . . . I stiffen at the thought that just went through my mind.

"Sara, are you still okay?" I didn't realize that he'd

stopped what he was doing when I stiffened up. I nod quickly so he would start back up again. "Habibti, what did I say, baby? No thoughts about anything but what I'm doing, yeah?" At my nod, again, he goes to my other breast and starts to repeat what he did to the left one.

It takes me only a brief moment to clear my head, and concentrate on what he was doing to my body. I never felt something so amazing as his mouth on my breast. Being blindfolded has my senses even higher, and I feel like I could come from the treatment he's giving my breast alone. I've always had to have clit stimulation to have an orgasm. This is new to me.

Just when I was about to come, he slows his treatment on my breast, and starts to trail nips and kisses down my stomach.

"Jesus, you smell so fucking good. I have to have a taste before I take you." I feel him settle between my thighs, which he puts on his shoulders. "I like the trail you left, baby," he murmurs against my lips before I feel his tongue lick me in one long swipe. My moan is muffled, but I can hear his moan of pleasure very clearly before he sucks my clit into his mouth. Holy shit! I'm unable to control the orgasm that takes over my body. It's hard and takes everything out of me.

"Fucking A, Sara. Give me another." He's slowly drawing out the last one I just had. This is causing me to slowly build into another orgasm that I feel coming much quicker than the last one. I'm not sure if I can handle another one, and I think this one is going to be harder and stronger. Shaking my head, I think about knocking on the headboard when I feel his finger enter me, and he slowly

starts to fuck me with it.

"I can feel it coming, Sara. Let it go, baby, so I can plunge into this velvet heat you have waiting for me." I feel his lips wrap around my clit, and he sucks hard. I detonate and scream into my gag. All I see is black, and I feel like I'm having an out-of-body experience.

"Open your eyes. I want to see your beautiful eyes as I enter you the first time." I slowly open my lids and realize he's above me with his hands on either side of my head. I didn't feel him when he moved nor did I feel when he removed the blindfold from my face. Glancing down, I see he's also undressed and has already put a condom on. He's slowly rocking his cock against the lips of my pussy and he hits my clit, which causes me to moan and jump.

I find his eyes again and stare into them. He slowly adjusts himself at my opening and pushes into me inch by inch. He's bigger than I've ever had, and the stretching causes me to wince a bit. Neil stops and waits until I nod at him to continue. Finally, after what feels like minutes, I feel his hips against mine.

"Fuck, you're so tight. How long has it been, Sara?" he asks as he removes the gag.

"A while. I've only ever had one partner, Neil." His face shows his shock at my statement. "I know. I make it sound like I have been sleeping with men, but I honestly haven't slept with anyone since I was seventeen, Neil." I close my eyes because I really don't want to talk about this right now. It's killing my mood because it's bringing back memories I don't want to remember.

"Fuck me. Thank you, Sara, for allowing me to have this moment with you." I feel his lips on mine, and he starts

to thrust slowly in and out of me. Jesus, he feels amazing.

I start to rock my hips and meet his thrusts. Ripping his mouth from my lips, and he stares into my eyes. "Mine, Habibti. You are mine. No more fighting this. No more," he growls out and then starts thrusting harder.

I can't take the look in his eyes anymore. The possessive look, the declaration, along with his thrusts getting harder, has me screaming out my pleasure and locking my legs around his waist.

"Sara, fuck, baby. Yes! Come on my cock. Milk my cum from me, baby," he whispers into my ear as he thrusts three more times and stills inside me as he erupts into the condom.

After a few moments, he unties my arms and they wrap around his body, holding him against me. I honestly don't know if I can take walking away from him in the morning. Rolling off me he, quickly takes care of the condom, grabs a towel and gently cleans between my legs. The towel is tossed into the corner of the room then he crawls into bed with me, holding me close to him.

"Get some rest, Habibti. Tomorrow, we can work it all out."

I close my eyes and pretend to fall asleep. I hope he isn't too pissed when he wakes up and finds that I'm not here. I just can't allow these feelings that are deep inside me to take over. His safety is more important to me than wanting to give this a chance.

"Sara, are you almost done? The new detective should be coming soon." Winters is outside the bathroom, and it causes me to come back to the present. I feel my face has tears sliding down it from the memory.

I quickly wipe my face and then clear my throat so I can answer her.

"Yep. I'll be out in a few moments. Thanks for the heads-up."

I shake my head and finish up with my bath. There's no way I can keep doing this to myself. No more memories of Neil. He's now my past, and I have to focus on what's going to happen when I'm moved from this house to the next safe house. It's time to forget these past seven years ever happened.

Twelve

NEIL

IT'S BEEN A TOTAL OF two weeks now that Sara has been gone and four days since I called Mace. Something has to give, and soon, because I'm not sure how much longer I can go without my heart. I need to make sure she understands she means more than anything to me; even more than my own life.

I glance back over at the letter that's sitting on my desk and feel the anger course through my veins again. I can't believe she thought I would buy that shit she wrote to me. It was less than five sentences, telling me that she never wanted to hurt our family or me and that I need to let her go. She wouldn't ever see us again, and it was better this way. That she isn't anything but a number to me now, so just let it be. For some reason, that sentence seems to stick out in my mind and I'm not sure why.

"Family dinner tonight, and you're coming." Ghost takes a seat in the chair in front of my desk. "Len isn't going to let you get out of it. Plus, Marcus wants to see his uncle for longer than fifteen minutes."

Glancing his way, I take a moment and let his words sink in. I adore my nephew, and with Len five and half months pregnant with twins, I know I won't get much time with him alone. Guilt runs deep in my stomach that I haven't been spending much time with him. I almost didn't have him in my life due to Len's kidnapper. I promised myself when I was holding him the first time that, next to my own wife and kids, I wouldn't ever put things ahead of my family again. But . . . wouldn't this situation be considered okay to put in front of them? I plan on Sara being that wife, so in a way, this is still doing things for my family. Right?

"All right. Have we heard from Mace? How are the other cases going?"

"Mace? Nope, haven't heard anything yet. I'm going to give him two more days before I check in. The rest of the stuff is going. Sin said they're working hard on finding the shit going on over there. He also mentioned he might stay longer. He wouldn't go into details, but I have a feeling it involves a woman." That last sentence has me taken aback.

Sin? What the fuck?

"Wait, are you sure?"

"His words were . . . 'Ghost, I'm planning on staying in town after all is done here. There's a situation that's needing my attention. I don't know what to make of it just yet, but I'll keep you updated.' Then, he hung up on me. If it was work related, he would've said. This only leads me to believe it's a woman," he sighs out the last sentence.

"Damn." That really does sum it up. Sin isn't one to chase after a woman. They chase after him.

"Dinner's at six. You don't need to bring anything but yourself." At my nod, he walks out of my office.

I guess it's time to face the family and the fact that it's going to be a bit longer before I have Sara with me at these dinners.

"He missed his uncle. No more waiting weeks before you spend more than a few moments, Neil." Len is trying to scold me. I think this is comical so I roll my eyes at my nephew.

"Little man, tell Mamma that Uncle Neil doesn't answer to her and that I'm trying to find your Auntie Sara so I can put my ring on her finger already." There's a collective gasp at my talk about marriage.

"You want to marry her?" Mom gently places her hand on my shoulder.

I hand Marcus off to my sister and sit back on the couch. The room's quiet, and all eyes are on me waiting to hear what I'm going to say.

"She's everything to me. I've known for a while that I wanted to marry her and that she was the one. I just wish now I'd told her how much she means to me. She means more than anything to me, and I need her in my life to breathe," the last comes out as a whisper.

"*Aktar men ayga.*"

My head snaps over to Ghost, and a small smile forms on my lips. He just said, "more than anything" in Arabic. It matches my nickname for Sara, and I know that's going to be the saying I say to her when I finally see her after this bullshit.

"*Ahebbouka aktar men ayga.* Thanks, brother, for reminding me." I hold my fist out for a bump.

"One of you want to fill the rest of us in?" Poppa Tony states from over on the couch.

"You know how Len and I say, '*Tl'mo, Len. Un'altra volta*' to each other? Well, in Arabic he calls Sara *Habibti* and it means *loved one. Ahebbouka aktar men ayga* means *I love you more than anything*," Ghost tells the room as he pulls Len closer to his side.

"That's beautiful, and I like how you boys want something that's just yours for the one you love." Pops stands up and walks over to Mom, giving her a peck on the forehead.

A small smile forms on my face. Pops has always kissed her there in front of others, and it always warmed my heart. Not that I would tell that to anyone, but it's nice to see my parents loving each other.

"Pops, why do you only kiss her on the forehead?" Squirt asks.

Mom gets a huge grin on her face and looks over at Pops, who is standing to the side of where she's sitting.

"I love your Momma with everything in me. I have no problem showing PDA, but I wanted to respect her and make sure I didn't maul her. By kissing her forehead, I'm showing her that respect, yet also showing her how precious she's to me."

This causes my sister to start crying. I roll my eyes because she seems to cry more these days. We missed her first pregnancy and didn't see her with these emotional outbursts. I'm not sure how Ghost handles this shit. I think for a moment if it will be that way with Sara.

"It will be. I want you to know that we love Sara and that we're okay with what you need to do to find her. If you need us, we're here," Pops tells me. I arch my brow at him because I'm not sure how he figured out what I was thinking.

"You said that shit out loud, pussy." Doc walks in and sits down next to OPG.

"James Reginald Hart, you watch your mouth when you talk about my grandson. One day a woman is going to knock you on your knees, and you're going to be the biggest pussy there is," OPG scolds him, which has the room chuckling.

"Bite your tongue, old woman. I won't be pussy-whipped ever. I like being able to play the field." He puffs his chest as he says this to her.

Off to the side, I see Ashley stand and walk into the kitchen. Everyone knows they have something going on, and I have a feeling he just got into deep shit with that comment. He quickly follows her, where I'm sure he's going to be kissing her ass trying to make up for that fuck up.

"I swear that boy should have been swallowed instead of conceived. He has no damn filter," OPG states under her breath but loud enough for everyone to hear. This has the room roaring in laughter within seconds.

"Jesus, Mom. I swear I'm going to get you non-alcoholic beer."

"Anthony, try it and see what happens."

"I would pay money to see you spank him, OPG." Carlo slaps his leg as he chuckles out loud.

"Don't encourage her, Carlo. Nicoli, put your money away already." Pops stands up and storms over to grab the money out of his hands.

Shaking my head, I stand to go give her a kiss on her

forehead and then head on out for the night. I have to give Mace a call tomorrow and hope he has some news for me.

Sara

Jesus. The past two weeks has dragged on. The detective that was supposed to come four days ago got delayed, and now we're really in need of supplies. We got a message from Conti that he's due to arrive today.

"Is this all you need?" Winters asks as she finishes the list of items that we need.

"Yeah, are you going to go to the store here in town and then drop things off before you take the days off you need to? What are your plans?"

"No. I'm going to the next town over. I'd rather not be seen much here." She stands up and drops the list into her purse, then makes her way back over to me and sits next to me. "Plan is to get some damn books. I need some reading material. Do you want me to pick up anything for you?"

Winters and I found out that we have an obsession with reading. We also like the same authors. She scoured my e-reader the other day and found some reads that she hasn't read yet.

"Doesn't KC Lynn, K. Langston, C.M. Steele, Cassia Brightmore, and Elena M. Reyes have new ones coming out? Shit, I miss the internet because I would be on that already. I know I had KC and K's newest ones preordered. But C.M. and Elena normally don't do that. Can you check? If they do, can you get them on your e-reader, then let me read them when you get back?"

"I know C.M. just released. I have a friend that's a ghost writer. Her name is Crystal. She follows all the authors we love. She doesn't write for them but she does write for a few others we love to read. She messaged me the other day with the link to purchase it because she knows I'm a huge fan. I'll tell you it's hot."

"What! Why haven't you let me read it yet?"

"It was on my phone. I plan on picking up my e-reader when I go out. I also have a surprise for you as well," she says with a smirk.

"Start talking, or no more eggs and bacon when you're here in the mornings," I threaten. She's an awesome baker but can't cook real food for shit, so normally I feed us when she's with me.

"That's just cruel," she says as I just arch my brow at her. "Fine, I'm getting you an e-reader under a fake name so you can read the new books."

"I could just kiss you right now. I swear if I wasn't straight, I would beg you to marry me. But sadly, I'm not into women. Even though you're hot."

She just cracks up at my antics. I think over the last two weeks; she's gotten used to the shit that spews from my mouth.

The knock on the door has us both sitting up straighter and glancing at it.

"Go to the room."

Leaving my bedroom door cracked a little bit so I can hear what is going on, I hide behind it.

"Can I help you?"

"Hey, I'm here for duty." I recognize that voice but can't place it. A chill slowly starts to go down my spine, and I get a feeling that something isn't good.

"I'm not sure I understand what you're saying. Duty for what?"

"I'm here to watch over Sara. I'm the new replacement."

"Credentials?"

I hear some movement, and then it's quiet. I take a moment to peek out of the crack, and what I see has me shaking my head. There's no way this can be true.

"Okay, come on in." Winters takes a step back and allows him to enter. He looks around the room as she shuts the door.

"Sara, come on out."

My legs are shaking, and I'm really not wanting to go out there. Conti wouldn't have allowed this. Something isn't right. I slowly start opening the door and see Winters walking my way. The moment she sees the look on my face, she rushes to my side.

"What's wrong?"

"I don't think he's supposed to be here, Winters," I murmur into her ear with my eyes locked on the man standing in the living room looking at me with a smirk on his face.

"What do you mean?"

"Ladies, come on in here. Let's get acquainted."

Quicker than I can blink, there's a gun pointing at both Winters and me. I knew something about him was off.

"Now!"

"What are you doing?" Winters questions.

"Walters. Why?" I ask. He shakes his head at me, and then points to the couch.

Oh, God, please don't let it end this way.

He allows us to walk in front of him, then I feel Winters being pulled back from me. I turn in time to see him cover her mouth with a rag and she immediately starts to struggle. I start to go to help her when the light hits the gun catching my eye. It's pointing at me again which makes me stop my movements. Winters slowly drops from his arms; unconscious.

"What did you do to her?"

"Don't worry your pretty little head. Go fucking sit down so I can explain what's going to happen now."

Taking steps backwards so I don't take my eyes off him, I slowly walk until I feel the couch hit the back of my knees. I take a seat and watch him as he drags Winters over to the radiator that's in the corner of the room. He quickly handcuffs her to it and takes her gun from her holster.

"Now that that's done, Sara, why don't we get to know each other better? Let's talk about why you're in hiding, huh?"

I shake my head because I really can't do this. Fear is coursing through my veins.

"I was so hoping this would be easy." He looks down at his watch and huffs out a sigh as he starts walking around the couch. "I have a few hours still left, and since you won't talk, then there's only one thing left to do."

His hand comes around, and raises the same cloth he held to Winter's mouth. No, I won't let him do this without a fight. I move forward but am stopped when I feel my hair being jerked back.

"No fighting, Sara. Take a deep breath. That's my girl." The cloth is forced over my mouth just as I start to scream. I smell something sickly sweet and start to gag. The feeling of sleep starts to consume me immediately and I try to fight it, but it's useless. Just as it starts to go black, he murmurs into my ear, "Diego can't wait to see you in person."

Thirteen

Rebecca

DEAR JOURNAL:

I meet him . . . the guy. The one from the last entry. He's way hotter in person than in a picture. He seemed to hate me from the first moment he saw me. But the feelings he provoked in me wasn't something I was used to. I have never felt these feelings before.

It's weird. I thought I understood love and what it meant to be in love. Arturo meant everything to me. He showed me what it was like to be in love and what it was like to have a family. So maybe this feeling isn't love. Maybe it's lust? But the thought of never seeing him again . . . just that thought alone has me gasping for breath and just wanting to die. I can't fathom him not being in my life. The weird thing is, I felt that way with Arturo. But it wasn't anything close to this strong. Is there a such thing as two different types of love? Can you have two people that you love with everything but feel different with each one?

God, this is so confusing, and I have nobody to really discuss this with. I'm alone in trying to figure this out because if I talk to the few friends I have made, then they will want answers. And answers aren't something I'm allowed to give them. I'm going to have to figure this out and figure it out soon. Because if I'm honest with myself, I can't afford to love someone right now. Not while they're still looking for me.

-Rebecca

I lay my head on the back of my chair as I clutch my journal to my chest. I don't know what I'm going to do with these feelings because I really can't afford to act on them. I close my eyes and just let myself imagine what a life with him could be like. It can't hurt to dream about this once, right . . .

Fourteen

Sara

MY HEAD'S POUNDING, AND I feel nauseous. It's like I've been drinking all night long.

Damn, Ashley, and her "girls need a night to party shit" she's always spewing monthly to us. It must have been a hell of a girls' night out if I'm feeling this way. It's going to be some time before I drink again. I wonder how the girls are feeling.

I slowly turn my head, and hope that I was smart and put aspirin on the side table. Just as I am about to open my eyes I hear male voices coming from somewhere.

What the fuck? Please, God, don't tell me I let a man in my home . . . well, from the sounds of it, more than one man.

"You said nothing about killing them."

I freeze as the memories start to flood into my mind just from hearing that one voice that's in the other room. Walters knocked Winters and me out. I wonder for a moment what room we're in. I'm assuming I'm in my room because I feel a bed under me. Cracking open my eyes slightly, I spot Winters next to me. I go to move my hand and realize we're handcuffed together. Her lids crack open and she slowly shakes her head no, telling me to stay still. Barely nodding my head at her, I close my eyes again and concentrate on the voices I heard.

"What in the fuck did you think we were going to do, Walters? Have a goddamn tea party and bake cookies with her? She saw something she shouldn't have seen and can put me and my men away for life. I can't have that shit. It's hard to do business from prison. Now, get the fuck out of my way or you will end up with the same fate as them."

Oh, God, that voice!

It's the same one from the bus . . . The same voice from that night so long ago.

"Diego, if you end me, then who are you going to have at the police station to help you out of all your shit?" Walters asks.

"You don't think I can find a replacement for you? You don't think I can buy off another police officer in a heartbeat? Don't fuck with me, Walters. Let's finish setting this up so we can get out of here. Boys, put it over in the corner. Set it for twenty minutes, and let's get the fuck out of here."

I feel a tug on my arm and crack my eyes open. Winter mouths "bomb" to me, and my heart starts pounding in my chest. How are we going to get out of this? The sound of footsteps nearing has my eyes closing quickly.

"Where you going?" Walters ask whoever it is.

"To make sure they're still out of it. We don't need them

waking and fucking shit up," a voice I don't recognize says.

The door to the room opens, and I try my hardest to slow my heart rate and act like I'm still out of it. I want to scream, and in moments like this, I normally would. I don't know what it is, but something is stopping me from doing it. A sense of déjà vu hits me, and I'm thrown back to another time that I felt this way. Tears threaten to start, but I have a sense of calm wash over me.

Momma. Daddy. Thank you.

The last time this happened, I could only think that it was my parents helping me through the fear and keeping me safe. I really didn't believe in ghosts or God much until then. Now, there isn't anything that can explain what is happening other than that.

After a few moments, I hear him walk away and say a quick prayer that it worked.

"Timer is set. Let's get the fuck out of here and far enough away to watch the explosion."

At the sound of the door shutting, I open my eyes and stare at Winters.

"Come on, Sara. We have to get out of here."

We sit up and see that we aren't handcuffed to the bed. I guess they didn't think we would wake up. She reaches into her pocket and comes up empty-handed.

"Shit, okay. They have my keys. We are going to have to work together. Come on." She tugs my arm as she's getting out of my bed. This is harder than what the movies make it look like.

We finally make it out of the bedroom and into the living room. Looking over to the side, I see the bomb they placed. I know nothing about these things, but I see the timer is slowly counting down and shows we have less than five minutes to get out of here.

"Okay, look—we need get out of here and as far away as we can before the bomb goes off. Make sure you keep up with me. We're going to run east."

She turns and tugs me out the door. Now would be a good time to tell her I don't know my directions really well.

"Winters, which . . ."

"Sara, there isn't any time. Come on." We aren't but fifteen steps out the door when we hear our names being called. This causes me to stop and turn in that direction. I see Conti about a block away running toward us.

"Conti, stop, there's a . . ." A loud explosion drowns out my voice, and I feel the impact of it behind me.

I'm flying into the air, and I feel a sharp pain in my right shoulder. Fuck. That isn't good. The impact of my body hitting the ground causes my head to slam hard into it. Immediately my vision is blurred and pain is going through my body. My ears are ringing so loud that even the pounding of my heart I was hearing is drowned out.

God, this hurts. Please don't let me die this way. I want to at least tell Neil I love him. Please . . .

I see a body hovering above me. Focusing my eyes, I see a man with caramel-colored hair, green, soft, kind eyes and he seems to be transparent. The overwhelming feeling of calmness comforts me. I have felt this before but always thought it was my mom and dad. Who is this man and what is he doing here with me? I feel darkness starting to seep into my mind, and I know I have to say it now before it's too late.

"Neil . . . love . . . please . . ." is all I'm able to get out before all I see is black and the sounds around me finally quiet down.

NEIL

Cracking my neck, I stand up and stretch. This day is dragging on, and I'm not sure if I'm going to make it through the rest of it. It's only ten in the morning, but it feels like I've been up for over twenty-four hours. Maybe because I haven't been sleeping well since Sara left.

I glance back over at the pictures that line my bookshelf. I put the ones she put in the box up there so I can see them daily. Once I get her back, I swear she won't be out of my sight again.

Before I realize it, I have her picture in my hand and I'm staring down at her beautiful face. My chest starts to hurt, and I realize it isn't from the tattoo that I ended up getting last night. It's the pain of not having her here.

"Hey, Mace called." Ghost, Doc, and Eagle walk into my office.

I turn toward them after I place the picture back in its spot.

"What's the update?"

"Sin's going to call in fifteen with it. Right now, he's faxing us all he has. From what Mace said, it isn't much right now." Eagle walks over to my pictures and looks at them. "You get what you needed to done last night?"

"Don't touch the pictures, fucker."

"Really? A picture, Lucky?" Eagle ask with an amused look.

I know it sounds fucked up, but even them looking at

her pictures right now pisses me the fuck off. I should have fucking hid them so nobody could look at them. At this rate, she'll be lucky to even be allowed out of the house when I finally get her back . . . okay, that's a lie. She would kick my ass if I tried to keep her locked up. Along with the girls.

"Sorry, I just miss her and need to find her soon. I can't keep this shit up, guys. It's killing me. I was bad when Len was missing, but this is hurting even more because I know she went willingly, if that makes sense. I mean, she knows we are security, but she still didn't come to us to protect her." I close my eyes and squeeze my hands into fists. It's time to hit the gym yet again today. This anger is hard for me to deal with, so I normally end up at the gym pounding a punching bag to get it out.

"What did you do last night after you left the house?" Ghost asks as he sits with a cup of coffee.

"I went and had some work done after I went to the gym."

"Work?" Doc hands me a cup of coffee and leans on the bookcase with his own cup.

"He went and saw Jeff. I was walking out when he walked in," Eagle says from the coffee pot in the corner of my office.

"Wait, why did you go to Jeff's?" Doc asks.

"I got some more added to my back piece," Eagle states.

"What did you get added?" Ghost asks Eagle.

"I'm curious, too, because your back is pretty much full."

"Got some more names from Boss."

"Shit," Doc murmurs and looks down. Yeah, that about sums it up. After that last mission, losing a brother has a new meaning. Don't get me wrong, it always hit home, but after that . . . it just makes it harder.

"Who?" Dante asks.

"Smith and Johnson." Damn, they were some amazing guys.

"Families?" Ghost asks.

"I'm in the process of getting some stuff set up today for the wives and kids," Eagle states, and we all just nod. That's something we all agreed on when we left. Help the families of the fallen brothers. We never want the families to go without. They will have a hard enough time dealing with the loss—we don't want them to have to struggle with anything else.

"Keep us informed."

I hear the fax machine going off and watch as Doc heads to the door to collect what Sin's faxing.

"What did you end up getting?" Ghost asks, as he gets up to get more coffee.

"Something for Sara. And no, you fuckers can't see it before her." There's no way they're going to see what I got done. She will see it first, even if I have to make sure it's covered for years; it will happen.

"Pussy," I hear coming from the phone in Doc's hand as he's walking in the door.

"Shut up, Sin. When the fuck you going to come home?"

"Umm . . . about that. I'm staying in Piersville for a while longer."

"Why the fuck are you staying?" Eagle asks the question we all are wondering.

"Because I fucking want to."

"For real, Sin, what's going on? This isn't like you," Doc states.

"Can't you all just leave it be?" he murmurs.

115

"John, I have to get going. I'm needed at the hospital," a girl's voice comes through the line. This has us looking at each other. Nobody calls him by his name.

"Babe, when you get off work, you get your ass back here." Then there's a loud smack sound and then a moan.

"Umm . . . Sin," Ghost chokes out behind his chuckle.

"Shit . . . *ma vie*, text me when you get there, then come back after work," we hear him murmur softly before the sound of a door closes. "Okay, so did you get the files?"

"You have some explaining to do, *ma vie*," Doc says sweetly into the phone.

"Later—right now we need to get this done. Now, fill us in. We got the fax. What did you find out about Sara?" My tone leaves no room for anything else.

"Honestly, there isn't much on Sara Marie Reyes. It's the same that we have there on file. The only thing that's new is there's some kind of connection with the name Rebecca Anne Bailey, who is deceased as of seven years ago. We're trying to pull up more info on who this Rebecca is."

At the name Rebecca, my chest tightens. Shit, that journal is Sara's, but, what does this Rebecca have to do with her?

"Thanks, Sin. If you find anything else, let us know ASAP," Ghost says staring at my face.

"What's up? You look pale as shit, and that happened when he mentioned the name Rebecca." Doc puts his phone on my desk.

I take a moment and explain about the journal and that I have been reading lately. I felt a pull to the person in it, but now that I know she's dead, I wonder why I felt that pull and how Sara's involved with this. The phone on my desk ringing grasps my attention when I see who it is. I didn't think I would hear from him again so soon.

"Conti, what's up?"

"Neil, get to Center Point. Sara was in an explosion and she needs you, now."

That's all I heard before I was out the door with my keys in hand. All I know is that I can't handle it if something happens to her.

Fuck, God, please don't take her from me before I get a chance to say I love you.

Fifteen

Sara

BEEP . . . BEEP . . . BEEP . . .

That's all I've heard for a while now. I have no clue what time it is or what day.

Beep . . . Beep . . . Beep . . .

This beeping is getting on my nerves. There's another buzz of noise in the background. I know I'm in the hospital, but I can't really remember why. I ache but can't move or open my eyes. I struggle to understand the other noise that's going on, and just when I'm about to give up, I make out that it's voices. Not just any voices either–I hear Dante, Conti, and Neil's.

Oh God, Neil.

"When are you going to tell us her story?" Dante whispers.

"It isn't something I can tell you. Honestly, I shouldn't have called you when she was on her way to the hospital. But, if I was in your shoes, I would want to know. If she decides to tell you when she wakes up, I can't stop her."

"Just tell me the people responsible are caught." Neil's voice holds despair in it, and my heart starts to pound at the thought that he's hurt.

The beeping noise starts speeding up and an alarm sounds. The sound of a door opening is followed by footsteps rushing in.

"What the fuck is going on?" My poor guy isn't taking this well from the sound of fear coming from him.

"Sir, calm down. Her heart rate is rising. It might be due to the pain she's in. It's time for more meds anyway," a female voice states.

"Well, give her something."

"Sir, if you don't calm down, you're going to have to leave. She doesn't need to hear this. She might not be awake, but I believe she cannot only feel the emotions in the room, but can also hear what is said."

I hear more rustling, and I start to feel the pull of the darkness again. I don't want to go back to sleep. I want to hear what's happening. However, my fight is for nothing, because before I can even take another breath, the black surrounds me again.

NEIL

I watch the nurse mess with the monitors again before she turns and heads out the door. Jesus, my poor girl has had a hell of a time. It has been thirty-two hours since she arrived at the hospital. Winters and Sara both had major concussions, cuts, and bruises from the blast. They both are lucky to be alive and with what the hospital considers "minor injuries." Even a bruise is too much for me to handle seeing on her.

I was at the hospital less than fifteen minutes after I got the call. I'll never forget seeing her being taken out of the ambulance on a stretcher the moment I reached the emergency room doors. Conti had to hold me back from beating the hell out of the nurse that refused to allow me back with her. After what seemed like hours, the doctor finally came out to tell us that she was going to be okay, and they had her in a medicated comma to allow her brain time to get the swelling down.

Len showed up shortly after that with the girls in tow. She talked with Chris, and both went to find out more answers. They came back shortly after that, Len with bloodshot eyes from crying, and explained that if her swelling doesn't go down in the next twenty-four hours, they would have to drill a hole to allow for the swelling to decrease. They stated Winters was in the same boat.

So far, we'd been lucky with Sara. Her swelling had gone down within ten hours, however, Winters had to have the holes drilled. Right now, there's an FBI agent in with her. I don't know the story, but I can see the same dread that has been on my face since I gotten that call.

"I'm going to go and check on Winters. Need anything?" Conti asks Ghost and me.

"I'll go with you. I need to call and check on Len."

They both walk out, and I scoot closer to the bed.

Grabbing Sara's hand, I lean my forehead on the joined hands. I just need her to wake up.

The sound of a phone ringing has me opening my eyes. Damn, I must have fallen asleep. I glance down and see it's Sin.

"Yo," my voice croaks out.

"Hey, how is she?" It's Sin calling to check in.

"Same."

"Did you find the connection between her and that Rebecca?"

"Shit, I haven't thought about it since you told us. You okay?"

"Yeah. If you need me, I'll be on my way back. Just say the word, man." I know he means it, but I also know that he really wants to stay. I don't know who this girl is but once things settle here, I'll get a name out of him and do some checking into things.

"Nah, thanks, though. I'll update you once I know more." I hang up and lean back in the chair. I really wish I knew the connection between Sara and Rebecca. I just find it odd that there was a journal labeled "Remembering Rebecca" in her drawer.

Staring at her face, I try to figure out how she would know her. Maybe it was a sister? Friend? There has to be a connection . . .

The thought of a line that was in the letter she wrote me floods my mind, and it starts to click together on why it stood out to me. I have read it before.

Grabbing the journal that somehow made it to the hospital with me, I look at the first page again, and there it is . . . *Just a Number*. I pull the letter from the back, and double check the last sentence. Sure enough, it matches. The writing, though, is different, but not by much. I turn to the next journal entry that I haven't read yet and . . . *Fuck me.*

Sixteen

Rebecca

DEAR JOURNAL:

I don't know how much longer I can keep my feelings from "him." I keep thinking about my past and know that once he finds out, he's going to be pissed that I've lied to him about everything . . . I don't know if I can handle seeing the look on his face. The look that I betrayed him and his family. I just can't.

The look he gave me this morning was bad enough. God, I wanted to cry and tell him how sorry I was for leaving him in bed alone. It was the hardest thing I have ever had to do. To see the hurt etched across his face by me breaking my word to wait for him to get up so we could talk about our "future." A future I want more than anything, but the thought of what I truly am, and why I am here . . . I can't put him in danger. It would end me to know he was hurt due to my past.

So . . . for now, I live in my memory of what it felt like to be in his arms. And I live with knowing that the love I have for him is much more than I ever felt for Arturo. I never stood a chance . . . Neil's everything.

-Rebecca . . . his *Habibti*

Seventeen

Sara

I FEEL MORE AWAKE THIS time around, and I also feel more pain. Damn, maybe being in the darkness is better. I take a moment, keeping my eyes closed, and take in the sounds. That damn beeping from the monitor is still loud, but I also hear a slight snore on the left side of me. The feeling of someone holding my hand has me slowly turning my head to the left and cracking my eyes open to see who it is.

I should have known it would be him. Taking in his appearance, I see that he has a beard going again and his hair looks like he has run his fingers through it over and over. His clothes are wrinkled, and it looks like he has been here for days. There's a white board right behind him on the wall, and I see it has been three days since . . . it's then that I remember the explosion and what happened.

Whatever noise I made must have been loud because I'm now in Neil's arms as he rocks me gently.

"*Habibti*, it's okay. You're safe now, love." This makes

me cry more. "Are you in pain? I need to get the nurse, but I need to know what's wrong, Sara," he murmurs in my ear.

"Winters?" is about all I can get out before I start to cough. My throat is dry, and I'm in dire need of water.

"She's here too. Let's get the nurse, okay?" He reaches over and presses a red button. Within minutes, a nurse is walking into the room.

"Ah, Ms. Reyes, you finally decided you had enough beauty sleep. How is your pain level on a scale of one to ten?"

"About a six. Can I have some water please?"

"Small sips for now. Let me go get the doctor to look you over, and we'll get you something for the pain." She walks out the door with a chart in her hand.

About forty minutes later the doctors have checked me over, and have cleared me to eat a liquid diet and to receive more pain meds. The whole time Neil wouldn't leave my side, and I'm glad he didn't. I couldn't stop staring at him because I didn't think I would ever get to see him again. How he knew about me being here, but I had no clue. Then again, he's in security and probably had my name flagged.

"Sara, we need to talk. I need to know what's going on. Conti said you would have to be the one to tell me. Before you say anything, you have to know something," he murmurs, then bends down and digs into a bag. His eyes are staring at me as he holds it up, "I know you're Rebecca. I know this is your writing. I read it." He's holding the red journal I know all too well.

Shame hits me as I know he has read about the thoughts I had of killing myself, of the addiction to the pain pills, of the fear and nightmares I've had, and the feelings I have for him.

"Jesus. Neil . . . I . . ." Tears start filling my eyes because I really don't want to tell him what happened.

"Sara, whatever happened, it isn't going to take my love for you away. *Habibti, ahebbouka aktar men ayga.* Before you even ask what that means, you tell me what happened. After that, I'll explain the words I just said, okay?"

I know he isn't going to let it go until I tell him everything. "Can you hold me while I tell you? I just need to feel you around me."

Without a second thought, he crawls up into the bed gently and adjusts me so I'm laying on top of him.

"Go on, love, I got you," he murmurs into the top of my head.

"Ten years ago, my world came crashing down . . ." And just like that, I'm transported back into my memories. To a time that I wish so hard I could forget . . .

Rebecca

Ten years ago . . .

The loud bang that came from our living room woke me up out of a dead sleep. I glance over at the clock and see it's five ten in the morning. I still have a good forty minutes before the alarm is due to go off. After last night's marathon of sex with Arturo, I was hoping to get at least three hours' sleep. I don't regret not getting enough sleep for work–after all, you only get engaged to be married once in your life. Okay, well it could happen more than that, but I was only planning for one time.

BANG.

What in the fuck? It sounded like a bomb went off in our apartment. Arturo jumps out of bed and rushes to our bedroom door. I can't see around him, but whatever he saw has him stiffening and turning back to me fast. Quickly he jumps back onto the bed with me and grabs my shoulders.

"Becs, hide and whatever you hear, do NOT come out of your hiding spot. Do you understand?" I don't move or make a sound. I just stare at him because I've never seen him scared before, and it has me trembling. "Becs, I mean it. You have to hide now. I love you."

He gives me a quick kiss on my lips before he's pushing me. The push is what I needed to get moving. The banging is getting louder and louder now, and I'm scared of what is going on. Do I scream? Can the neighbors hear? Will they call the police?

I tumble off the side of the bed and lie as flat as I can on the floor. Our mattress is close to the floor, but I have been under it before getting shoes so, I squeeze as much of my body as I can between the bed and the ground. I only succeed in fitting about a third of my body under it. I don't understand why I can't fit under the bed any more than I can.

"Get the fuck in here now." I don't recognize this voice at all.

The blanket from the bed flies off and covers me completely. Deep down, I know Arturo did this on purpose to protect me. I see a flash of light in the room and a loud bang that I know for sure is a gun. My mouth opens to scream, but nothing comes out. My body feels like something is sitting on it, and I feel as if a hand is covering my mouth. A sense of

S. VAN HORNE

calm rushes through me and reminds me to stay still and not make a sound.

"Everyone in here? Good, now where's the drugs and money?" The voice is deep and sounds as if it belongs to someone who is not in control of their thoughts. Well, like a crazy person.

"I don't know . . ." Three loud bangs sound and I squeeze my eyes shut at the screams that come from the other room.

"Again, where are they?"

"Look, this is my apartment, and I have no clue what you're talking about," Arturo explains.

"Say goodnight." A loud bang sounds, but no scream follows. Just moans of pain from the others.

"Last time . . . where are the drugs and money?" the voice demands. For the rest of my life, that voice will forever be etched into my brain.

Nobody answers, and I start to shake at the thought of what's going to happen. I have no clue what they're looking for but I imagine they have the wrong apartment. Quickly, I say a prayer that the cops can get here fast enough to catch them and help the boys because I know they've been shot. I just don't know how badly.

The room is suddenly filled with the sound of gunshots firing one after the other. I see flashes of light that must be coming from the guns as they're being fired. Screams of pain and agony are coming from the boys, and I pray for it to end quickly. Still, I don't make one sound or move one muscle. But I can't stop the tears flowing down my face. After what seems like hours, the shooting stops and it's dead silent besides the agonizing moans of pain.

Slowly, I get up from my hiding spot and look out the

door of our room. There's nothing there. I can smell the gunshot residue in the air, but I pray this is just a horrible dream. Surely nothing like this can happen to someone like me. I walk to the door frame and take a look around.

The door to our apartment is shattered on the floor, and I see the neighbors starting to fill the hallway outside the door. I glance around the room and see bullet holes sliced into the walls, and my stomach clenches, knowing this isn't just a horrible dream. This is a real-life nightmare.

The sounds of moans have me looking at the two men who are on the couch. Rupert is covered in blood, and I see it pouring out of his chest. Mauricio is shot too, and part of his right leg is missing.

God, this can't be happening.

At my feet, I spot Arturo and I bend down to see his head is covered in blood and there's a hole in the back. I drop to my knees beside him, cover my face with my hands and sobs burst through.

I can't see any more. Please, God, just wake me up.

"Becs, help me please," Mauricio cries out from the couch. I jump up quickly and rush to the phone dialing nine-one-one while helping him with his leg.

"Nine-one-one, what is the situation of your emergency?"

"Please, send someone. My apartment was broken into and my fiancé, his brother, and friend were shot. Please hurry! They're bleeding badly," I sob into the phone just as Mauricio screams out in pain from me moving his leg.

"I'm sorry. I'm trying to help you. I'm sorry I hurt you," I murmur to him, trying to soothe him.

"Ma'am, how many are shot, and are they alive?"

"Three are shot. Two are on the couch and they're breathing. My fiancé isn't moving. Please . . . you have to help him."

I drop to my knees by Arturo and try to get him to wake up. Nothing is happening. I can't hear anything anymore except the ringing in my ears because I know deep down, I know he's gone.

"Ma'am, you need to move so they can work on him," I hear a voice by my ear. Looking up, I realize that the police are here. They took the phone out of my hands, and now are trying to get me away from Arturo.

I'm pulled to the side of the room and watch as they turn Arturo over and begin working on him.

"He's DOA. His heart is only four beats a minute. Let's move to the others."

I hear someone screaming *no* at the top of their lungs and realize it's me that's doing it. Dropping to my knees, I just continue to scream and cry because my life just ended right along with Arturo.

"Rebecca, I'm Detective Conti. Come with me. Let's get you out of here."

Sara

Present . . .

I close my eyes tightly against Neil's chest.

"I was interrogated for hours until finally they realized that I truly didn't know much. Rupert died the day after the shooting, and Mauricio died five days later. I found out the flash of light I saw in the bedroom was them shooting the bed. It was inches from where I was hiding. If I would've made it under the bed all the way, I would've been shot." I take a deep breath and continue. "I ended up in a mental hospital for depression for a week. My nerves were gone. We found out later that Mauricio was a drug dealer, and they were after him for encroaching on their territory. About three weeks after the shooting, an article came out about it and described a young woman being in the apartment. My name was never revealed. However, the day after the newspaper came out, I was on the bus and I overheard three guys talking about how they had to find and get rid of me. I contacted Conti, and I was put into witness protection. The people I picked out of a photo lineup that were on the bus happen to be part of the Mexican drug cartel."

I feel his hands caress my back. I'm done talking. I have nothing left in me to give. Just as I feel sleep pull me under, I swear I hear him say, "*Habibti,* don't worry. You'll never have to face it again."

NEIL

Sara shudders again in her sleep. My arms tighten slightly, letting her know that I'm still here, and she relaxes yet again. She ended up crying herself to sleep when she finished telling me her story. I'm glad she never looked up at my face while she shared her past with me. The fear and dread that poured out of her body, along with her words, was enough to make me want to murder someone. I felt every frightened tear that came from her eyes as she relived that night.

A tear falls from my eye at the thought that my beautiful, brave woman has faced so much in her short time. Nobody should ever have had to see what she'd witnessed. I now get why she kept her silence.

Part of being in the program is that they can't tell anyone who they really are. If they do, they risk being taken out of the system. I know that if it gets out that she told me, her protection from them is in jeopardy, and my family's lives are placed in danger. This means I'm going to have to have a talk with Conti about knowing. I do know that she isn't going to be out of my sight anytime soon. She will be leaving the hospital with me when she's discharged.

The knock on the door has me holding on to Sara a little tighter. Ghost pops his head in, and seeing the look on my face, doesn't even think twice about walking in with Doc and Eagle following. As they settle in, I know me telling them puts her protection even more at risk, but there isn't anyone else I would trust with her safety than the few in front of me.

"What happened?" Doc asks.

"Jesus. I don't even know where to begin. All I know right now is that my heart hurts, and I want to do everything in my power to make sure she's safe and with me at all times." Rubbing her back, I begin to tell them what she told me.

"Mexican cartel? Fuck me. You know this isn't good. It depends on how high these guys are. Did she give you a name?" Eagle asks as he writes down what I explained to them.

"Diego Garcia. He's a low-level drug pusher. He was told from the higher-ups to get this taken care of, or they will. Honestly, if we can get him alive, it helps the DEA and FBI in taking the cartel down. That's why her testimony is needed. It's just her and another witness," Conti says from the door. "They don't know about the old woman that lived down the hall that saw them leave." He takes another deep breath and looks me straight in the eyes. "You do know that now that you all are aware of the situation, her protection is compromised. However, I don't plan on telling many that you know because we could use your help in protecting her. Walters isn't the only bad cop that knew about her. Until we find the mole, we can use all the help we can get."

"Anything for Sara," Doc murmurs all of our thoughts.

"We protect everyone, but we take protecting our own even more seriously. And that's what Sara is, even if she wasn't this fucker's woman." Ghost points at me.

"Is that what she is? Yours?" Conti asks with his brow arched. I don't know if this fucker is asking due to being protective of her, or because he wants her for himself.

"Why are you questioning it? If it's because you want her, get that thought out of your damn head because I won't let her go. I wasn't letting her go when you dropped off that letter, and I'm not letting her go now even if I do know her story," I growl because I really don't want to beat his ass, but I will when it comes to someone trying to take her from me.

"Calm down. She's like my sister. I've come to love her over the years, but nothing in the intimate way. She's alone in the world, and I don't want her alone anymore. I urged her to make friends, and I've kept an eye on her even when she didn't know I was watching. I like you for her, but I'll warn you; you hurt her, I'll kick your ass and bury you where you will never be found. You being a Seal doesn't scare me." He tells me the last part staring me right in my eyes. I admit that takes guts, but I'm glad to hear that it's strictly for a sisterly love that he has for her and that he's being protective.

"So, what's the plan for after she's released?" Ghost brings up the question that I'm sure most in this room are wondering.

"She'll be going home with me. Eagle, double check the security at my home to make sure it's up to date. Also, add extra cameras outside my property line. Doc, find all you can on this Diego person. Also, call the twins, they can help with digging up information from Italy. Ghost, make sure Len is safe and our family is also protected. Conti, I guess you will be staying with us at the house." I glance back down at the woman in my arms. She's worth everything, and so the extra that I'm doing may seem like it's overkill, but I refuse to let these assholes get her.

I watch everyone starting to file out of the room and look up to see Conti leaving out the door last. Right before he shuts the door, he says something that has my breath clenching in my chest.

"For the record, she loves you so much, Neil. She cried herself to sleep nightly while she was in the safe house and would whimper out your name. Once, she woke up crying saying that it was you they shot in the nightmare. She told me that she would rather die than see you dead. I hope you realize what you have in her because some of us would give anything to have what you have in your arms."

Eighteen

NEIL

IT'S BEEN A WEEK SINCE Sara was brought into the hospital. Even though she only needed a few days, the doctors and Conti agreed for safety, as well as medical reasons, that staying a few more days would be good. We'll have to watch her closely for a few months to make sure that there are no lasting effects from her brain swelling, but they're hopeful there's no lingering issues that we might have to face.

Today we're taking her home—finally. We have a plan worked out with the hospital. They're going to state she's still a patient and will discharge her in two days, that way she's situated at home before the cartel knows she's out.

"Neil, really, I don't think it's wise I stay at your house. I can't have you and the family at risk. Just let me go to the safe house."

She has been saying this for two days now. I don't think she's understanding that she's mine and that I refuse to let her out of my sight.

"*Habibti*, this is the last time I'm going to express this. You're coming home with me. Conti even agrees that it's safer because they aren't expecting you with anyone but the Marshals. So, stop before you piss me off." I'm hoping the look on my face is enough to make her realize that things are going the way we have worked it out.

"Neil," she sighs out.

Fuck this.

I storm over to her, grabbing the back of her neck and slamming my lips down on hers. She stiffens for just a moment before she melts into the kiss. Damn, I missed her taste. I lick her lips, demanding entrance, and she complies quickly. Sweeping my tongue across hers, I fuck her mouth like I want to fuck her body. After a few moments, I slow the kiss down and pull back only enough to get her to listen.

"Sara, love. You're going home with me. No more arguing. I still have to talk with you, and the sooner you stop spewing the bullshit and arguing with me, the sooner we can talk and then I can worship your body," I murmur against her lips.

"Okay," she says on an exhale.

"Good. Now shake that ass and let's go." I kiss her on the forehead and step back from her. I guess that snapped her out of her fog because she gives me a dirty look and narrows her eyes at me.

"You did that shit on purpose," she hisses between her teeth.

"Don't know what you're talking about. But you agreed, so let's go." I turn and walk out the door to find the doctor. Hell, yeah, I did that shit on purpose, and I don't regret it either. Now that I know for sure it works, she will be getting a lot more of that when I want to get my way.

Pulling up the drive, I glance at her off to my right. Not many people have been in my home. However, I've been slowly decorating it with her in mind, but I'm not sure if she's going to like it.

When I started building it, the thought of her in my home is what drove me to design it the way I did. I dropped hints and would ask her questions on what she thought of looks or appliances. Showed her pictures of tiles, wall color, windows, doors . . . all the while making sure I watched her expressions so that I picked the one I knew she would really like. She always asked why I was asking her opinion, and I blew it off as just curious to what she would pick.

"This is yours? Why haven't I seen this place?"

"It wasn't finished until recently. You ready?"

She gets out of the car gently, and I remind myself that it might be a few more days before I can sink into her. I know she's still sore from the explosion, and as much as I want to make her mine for good, I know she needs to fully heal first. That's something every alpha type man will agree with. We won't do anything to risk our woman's health, even if it means suffering from blue balls for the rest of our lives.

After I guide her up the steps, I quickly open the door and unarm the alarm. As I reengage it, I turn and watch her take in my home. It's three levels; the main level, upstairs, and then the basement which is also a safe room.

The safe room has three bedrooms, kitchen, living room, two bathrooms, and a game room of sorts. I honestly don't go down there much. It's really for safety if something was to come up.

The main level holds the living room, my office, kitchen, two half-baths, media room, and game room.

The upstairs has four bedrooms and each one has a full bathroom. One of them I turned into a gym for now, and the other two are guest rooms. The master is the biggest of all and has a balcony with a coffee station along the back area that's covered from the weather, and a mini fridge under it with drinks. I spend most of my mornings and nights out there reflecting on things now that I've officially moved in.

The whole house is decorated in a modern-day look except the kitchen, which is decorated in soft blues and yellows. Squirt, Mom, and Momma Gio helped me with decorating after I stated I was going to marry Sara. They took over after hearing I decided white was a good look for everything. I glance around again and realize I was wrong—white sucked.

Turning back to Sara, I continue to watch her look around and take everything in. Whatever she doesn't like, she can change it. After all, this is our home now.

"What do you think?"

"I like it a lot, Neil. You did good." She has a tight smile.

"What's wrong? If you don't like something, we can . . ."

"Who decorated?"

"What?"

"This has a woman's touch. I was just curious which girlfriend decorated?" It takes me a moment to realize she's jealous. This causes me to chuckle out loud, which makes her narrow her eyes at me.

"Never mind. Just tell me where the guest room is. I

want to lie down." She turns to head upstairs.

Immediately, I sober my laugh and clench my hands into fists.

"Stop." At my command, she turns slowly to face me.

"Excuse me?"

"Stop and listen. Len, Mom, and Momma Gio decorated for me. No one other than family has been here. Not even the guys at work. I wanted you to be the first to see it before they did. So, get that shit out of your head. I haven't been with a woman since that first time I saw you, years ago at Christmas. Like I already I told you, Sara, you're it for me, *Habibti.* You're not sleeping in a guest bed because you're going to be sleeping in the master bedroom, in *our* bed. I built this house with you in mind. Don't you recognize the tile on the floor, or the bay window right over there?"

Sara

Shit, he's right. I do recognize all that stuff.

I recognized it immediately which made my breath catch in my throat. I couldn't believe that he took my preferences and added them into his house. And, I'll admit, they all look amazing together. Then when I saw the pictures on the walls, I knew he didn't decorate and a woman had to have done it. The thought of some other woman being the one do it and not me made the feeling of jealousy run through my blood.

Wait . . . did he say our bed?

"What do you mean our bed? Neil, this isn't my house!"

"Jesus, when are you going to get it, Sara? You're *MINE.* Didn't you just hear me say I built this house with you in

143

mind? I think it's time for a talk. Let's get you into bed and comfortable, then we'll have this discussion that I'm realizing is long overdue." He gently takes my hand and guides me up the stairs.

When we reach the landing, he turns to the right and enters the double doors that are a few feet away. I slowly follow him and take in the room. It's breathtaking. There's a huge, king-sized four-post bed in the center of the room that I have no clue how I'm going to get into because it's so high off the floor. A nightstand is on each side of it, and then across from the bed is a huge armoire dresser. Next to it is a vanity that any woman would die for. There's a door next to it, and I assume that would be the bathroom. To the right of the bed is floor-to-ceiling windows and a sliding door that opens to a balcony that's the length of the room. There's a cove that's covered with a door on it. To the left of the bed are two sets of double doors that make up the whole wall.

I walk over to the doors, open one, and see it's a walk-in closet full of Neil's stuff.

Dear God, I could live in this closet.

Turning my head, I give him a look with an arched brow. With a shrug, he nods at the other set. Shutting the doors, I walk over to the other set and open them. My breath catches at the sight of all my stuff from my apartment being here.

How and when did he do this?

"After Conti dropped off your box that you sent me, I went to your house, got all of the stuff that was yours, and brought it here. I placed everything where I though you'd want it. You'll probably move it to another spot, but at least your stuff is here," he explains, and I figured I must have said my question out loud.

Taking a few more moments to look at the closet, I gently shut the doors and just stand there trying to take it all in. I'm not sure what he's wanting me to say or how to react to someone just taking over. I had to rely only on myself for so long that I'm not sure if I can just allow someone to take over. Especially with my safety. Even in the safe house, it was hard for me to just let go and trust them.

I feel the heat of his body press up against my back, and I stiffen in response. That slight move has my muscles tightening up, and pain shoots through me. It isn't as bad as when I first woke up in the hospital, but I'm still pretty sore. It causes me to groan, and Neil immediately puts his arms around me to stop me from leaning toward the doors in front of me. It's about time for more medicine, but I don't want to take more of them. I don't like the way it makes me feel, and I know we need to talk still.

"Come on, *Habibti*. Let's get you to bed and get you some medicine. I have a heating pad if you want." He guides me to the bed.

"And just how to do you expect me to get into said bed, Neil? I swear you picked out the biggest bed so I couldn't run away once I got into it."

Chuckling, he bends down and pulls out steps that were hidden under the bed. Well, damn—he thought of everything, didn't he?

"Why so big?" I mumble as I slowly make my way up the steps and into the huge bed. I immediately fall in love as I slowly sink into it. It's like sleeping on a cloud. It isn't too hard, but it isn't so soft that you sink all the way into it. "Oh God, I may never leave this bed."

"And that's exactly why I got it. I knew you'd love it." He

bends again, and I'm assuming he's putting the steps away.

"Wait . . . I might need to get out of bed. So I need you to leave it there for me."

"I'm not leaving your side, so you won't need it. Plus, I like your idea of not being able to run. Now, let me go get your meds, some food, and something to drink." He turns and walks out before I can respond.

After a few moments, he comes back with some soup, a bottle of water, and my medication. I slowly sit up against the headboard and watch him as he sits beside me and starts to feed me some soup.

"I'm going to feed you and explain a few things. Then we'll get you your meds and hopefully you can get some rest." He holds up another spoonful, and I nod my head at him to continue.

"After that Christmas I first saw you, I went back to Cali and couldn't stop thinking about you. I kept trying to figure out what I was feeling when I saw you standing there watching my family welcome me home. It took some deep analyzing and some years before I realized the feelings I was experiencing were because I wanted you. From that moment, I stopped seeing other women. I started thinking about how I could make you mine. Jesus, Sara, I tried everything to get you to notice me. Yeah, I'm an asshole, but I didn't know how to make you see that with you, I would be anything you ever needed me to be." He continues to feed me the soup until it's gone.

"Okay, but that doesn't explain the house. Why didn't you just tell me when you moved back to Kansas City?" I grab the bottle and meds from him and take them. I know we have about fifteen minutes before they will start to kick in.

"I didn't know how because of the fear that you didn't feel the same way . . ." He stops speaking for a moment before starting again. "I figured if I could build you a house and show you that I was committed to taking care of you, that maybe you might open up to me finally. I knew you were hiding something but I didn't know what that was. Then, Len was taken. I had to get my sister back." He glances out the windows and is quiet for a moment.

"Neil?"

"I was afraid you wouldn't believe me when I said I would keep you safe, since she was taken when I was there. I even questioned myself. Then, the cabin happened. Sara, that was the best moment of my life. Waking up alone scared me, and made me realize that you didn't trust me. That you didn't want the same thing. After that, what happened again with Len in the other cabin . . ." He looks down and grabs my hand.

"I knew you wouldn't trust me again with your safety. So, I tried to show you other ways. I had cameras put into your home and I had someone follow you to make sure you were safe. I even sometimes would sneak into your home at night just to check on you. I know it sounds stalkerish, but I just had to make sure you were okay."

It really does sound like he's some damn obsessed stalker. But then there's a small part of me that's flattered in a way that he needed to make sure I was safe. A horrible feeling washed over me because I didn't trust him with my secret at that time. But I didn't want him or his family in jeopardy. And if I did tell, I could have lost my witness protection status.

"Neil, it wasn't you that I didn't trust. Yeah, I get what

you're saying, but you need to realize that I didn't want your family to get hurt from my past. I wouldn't have been able to live with myself if I knew you were hurt due to me. Also, you know that if I told anyone and the detectives found out, I would've lost my safety."

"I know that now, but then I didn't." He takes a deep breath. "I decided at the party that I was done. I needed to get you to talk to me and open up. Then you got the call and left. I can't express the pain I felt of not seeing you and not knowing where you were and if you were safe. I ended up telling my family that you were it and I had to find you. That you're worth more than anything in this world to me. Even more than my family."

The last word is whispered and has me gasping. Everyone knows that Neil loves his family fiercely and that he puts family above all. For him to say that speaks numbers to me.

"Neil . . ." I barely speak his name to tell him not to say that, but he puts his finger on my lips, stopping all thoughts, and stares deeply into my eyes.

"*Ahebbouka aktar men ayga, Habibti,*" he murmurs before gently placing a kiss on my lips and pulling away. "*I love you more than anything, my love*, is the translation from Arabic."

The burn in the back of my throat has me realizing that the tears are falling down my face. He slowly wipes them away and gives me his signature smirk.

"So, now you know. I'm addicted to you, and I'm not just talking about your taste either. I'm addicted to the taste of your sweet pussy like a crackhead needing his next fix." With his smirk in place, he continues. "And, baby, you have had me waiting for months for my next fix. We need you resting so you can heal, and I can have you again."

His analogy has me laughing.

"I love that sound," he murmurs, then leans in and places a small, sweet kiss on the corner of my mouth. Pulling back, he searches my face again. He must like what he sees because he then crashes his lips on mine and thrusts his tongue into my mouth. He's fucking it like he did my body that night back in the cabin. I'm surrounded by his smell, touch, and taste which pulls me into a fog that's all Neil. I don't know how long he kisses me, but I finally feel him breaking it, and I'm sucking in much-needed oxygen that I didn't realize I was lacking.

"*Habibti*, go to sleep and get some rest."

"Will you hold me until I fall asleep?"

"Anything you want, baby, it's yours." He climbs up behind me and carefully holds me around my waist, being mindful of my aches that I'm slowly not feeling anymore due to the pain meds. But I secretly wonder if part of the reason I'm not so sore anymore is because Neil finally told me he loved me.

"Shit," I grunt out and quickly try to turn toward him. "Neil . . ."

"You okay? Did I hurt you?" The panic that's in his voice makes my heart skip a beat knowing that he's worried that he caused me pain.

I glance up into his eyes. "No, I just need to tell you something." I take a deep breath and try to convey with my eyes as much as I can just how deep he affects me while I gather the right words.

"Sara, whatever it is can wait until you wake up."

"Neil, shut up," I growl at him, which causes him to throw his head back and laugh loudly. Neil's hot when he's brooding, but when he's laughing and smiling, it's breathtaking and makes you lose all train of thought. I'm staring at him when he brings his eyes to mine and I see the humor and light shining through them.

"Sara, I love the growl, but, babe, you need to remember something. The bedroom—that's my territory, and I call the shots in here. Now, sleep." He tries to turn me again which snaps me out of the fog that I seem to be in often with him.

"No, listen. When I was flying in the air . . ." I take a deep breath again because my throat feels like it's going to close again. "I had only one thought go through my head. I wasn't sure if I would ever see you again and knowing that I never told you how I truly felt. Neil . . . I love you more than anything, too."

I feel his body move up and down, which tells me that he's laughing. As I start to pull away from him, pissed that he would respond that way, he laughs harder and holds me closer to him.

That fucking asshole!

"Sara. *Habibti*, I know you love me, too. You said so in your diary and when you were coming in and out of consciousness at the hospital. Now, go to sleep."

"Still, laughing when I'm finally saying it out loud and will remember doesn't mean you should laugh."

He stops laughing and leans above me. Staring down into my eyes, he gives me that smirk that I would really love to hate but can't.

"I know, but you're so high on drugs right now that I'm not sure if you'll remember this. Now, go to sleep and tell me again when you wake up." He gives me another soul-searching kiss that leaves me breathless, then tucks me again into his arms.

With a small grin, I start to fall asleep. I could have sworn right before I was out for good I heard him say, "You really do mean more than anything to me, Sara."

Nineteen

Sara

IT'S BEEN A MONTH SINCE I was released from the hospital, and still nothing. They can't find Diego. It's like he disappeared. I'm getting tired of being stuck in the house with nothing to do. I'm not allowed to go out, but I can work from Neil's, I mean *our*, home. He also has been working from home too. He hasn't let me out of his sight since we got home from the hospital. Everyone has been bringing whatever we need to us.

Yeah, I've had some visitors checking in, but I need some time out of the house. It pisses me off that I'm stuck, yet again, inside a house and not able to do much. Hell, Neil won't even touch me yet. Even though I'm healed, I still have bruises that are fading way too slowly. I tried to get him to ignore them and have sex with me. Even went as far as having the doctor tell him that I'm fine. But nope, he takes one look at my yellow-green spots and stops. I'm so beyond sexually frustrated that I swear I'm about to explode.

I need to talk to the girls. No, what I really need is a

night out on the town with them. Then a thought hits me, and I know I have to act fast before Neil gets done in the shower. I quickly text the girls telling them what I'm in need of and tell them that I'm deleting the text so Neil won't see it. After a few moments, my phone goes off, alerting me they got the message.

Julia: *Yes, on it girl.*

Len: *Done. Deleting after all replies.*

Ashley: *About time bitch! We have been waiting for you!*

Andy: *I've got the tic tacs! Deleted <3*

Andy's text has me giggling out loud. That man and his Tic Tac challenge.

I hear footsteps coming down the hallway, so I quickly delete their replies and place the phone on the table in front of me. I pick up my e-reader and start to read K. Langston's newest book, *The Detective's Trust.*

"Good book?" he murmurs as he kisses the top of my head.

"I think it's her best yet. Good shower?" I put the e-reader on the table and turn toward him just as his phone pings with a notification.

I see his brow furrow, and then he shakes his head and taps furiously on his phone. Sitting back, I feel a smile start to form on my face. They're fast.

"Fuck . . . Sara, the girls want time with you. The guys are on my ass because we haven't allowed them to have a girls' night in forever. And Len is pulling her 'I'm pregnant with twins and I need girl time before I'm stuck with three kids under the age of two,'" he grunts. He narrows his eyes at me. "Why are you smirking? Did you know they were up to this?"

Shit.

"Um, no?"

"Are you asking me or telling me no?"

"Telling?"

"*Habibti,*" he growls out between clenched teeth.

"Well, I might have mentioned going stir crazy."

Sighing, he walks over to me, sits down, and drags me into his lap.

"You guys can go with us, but we want to be left alone to catch up. I'll be safe, and I will not leave your sight."

After a few moments of watching my expressions, he finally groans and nods his head.

"I love you, Neil," I say against his neck, then give him a kiss there.

"I love you too, *Habibti.*"

I try to contain my smile a bit, but I'm so damn excited that I'm getting out of this house and going to hang with everyone. Tonight will be epic.

"You're gay?" There's no way this guy is gay. He's so damn hot. He has to be fucking with us because we're well past drunk—well, everyone but Len and our men who are on watch.

"Why is it so hard to believe that I'm gay? I mean, look at these two," he says and points at Andy and Chris. "They're hot."

"Yeah, but they're Andy and Chris. You're a model!" The girls nod their heads in agreement, and Ashley even throws in an *Amen* for good measure. Which then causes model-hottie to laugh at us.

"Well, thanks for that, I guess," Chris murmurs, shaking his head at our logic.

We met the model-hottie shortly after we got here, and hit it off. I decided that next time I talk to Winters, I'm going to have to tell her about him because her ghost writer friend needs to know about this guy. An idea hits me and I grab my phone, taking his picture and typing away a text to Winters with his name and how to find him on Facebook.

"What are you doing now?" Andy looks over my shoulder.

"Sending this info to Winters for her writer friend. I think he should be on book covers," I murmur out.

"Oh wait! We can test the Tic Tac theory! Where's my box? Baby, did you bring it in with you?" Andy drunkenly turns toward Chris and in the process almost falls out of his chair. Chris quickly rights him—he's also sober but it seems he's enjoying our stupidity.

"No, I left them at home. I told you that you were NOT going to bring them and have strangers see how many they can swallow." Chris is rolling his eyes by the time he stops talking.

"But, babe! I had them customly, wait is that a word? Yes, I say it's a word because it makes sense. So, they're customly made! I even had a website made for people to report their findings, too. I need you to go get them you—complete llama collector," he screams and points to the door.

"Oh God you have been using that app again haven't

you? And no, not happening."

"Wait, what is this Tic Tac challenge?" Rome asks.

We watch his face as Andy, who is trying to explain what is happening but slurring horribly, tell our newest friend, Rome, the theory behind the swallowing Tic Tacs.

"Okay, you got me intrigued now. I'm going to have to keep an eye on this website." He then turns back to Ashley. I'm beginning to wonder if he isn't bi because he keeps looking over at her.

"Okay, why are you staring at our girl?" Andy pipes up from beside me.

"I just can't figure it out. Have we met before? I moved here from Pascagoula, Mississippi," he asks her.

"Nope, I've never even heard of that place," she slurs.

"It's just weird. I know you from somewhere."

"I just have a common face, is all."

At the mention of face something flashes in his eyes, but I'm too drunk to even register what it means.

"You're have more than a common face, you—tea-bagger, and you know it," Andy says and turns toward Chris, but he ends up almost falling off the stool again.

"You're cut off, from not only that damn application, but also from drinking. I think you're drunk enough. I don't need you getting sick in the morning."

"Wait, we need one more toast, then no more," Julia says and waves the waitress over. We've been getting crazy with our toasts to each other. Each one had something to do with pussy, cocks, or orgasms. I had a plan—I was going to get Neil to sleep with me tonight, no matter what.

"Who is doing this one?" Len asks as she sips her Diet Coke.

"I got it this time. But I have to ask what the name of the site was you made up, Andy?"

"Well, it's under construction, but it's www.hmttcys.com. It stands for how-many-Tic-Tacs-can-you-swallow. I'm going to have it where people can enter their amount. Chris said I couldn't ask if they were straight or gay. So, I guess it's now just a 'how many can you swallow challenge.'" He turns and pouts at Chris.

This causes us all to start howling in laughter because we know he would demand that answer if Chris wasn't stopping him. He just shakes his head at us and walks over to the boys that are off to the side shaking their heads with him. The waitress comes and drops off the Lemon Drop shots we have been doing all night.

"Okay. Raise your drinks." We all raise our shots. "I want to be naughty and still be nice, I want the fun without the price, I want the thrill of a long-drawn kiss, I want the things that good girls miss. I want the lights that brightly shine, I want the men, I want the wine. I want the arms and heart of a man, and still stay single if I can. Now, what I want is a little advice, on how to be naughty and still be nice!"

We toss our drinks back, and I find Neil's eyes staring at me with his smirk in place.

"Okay, party's over now," Chris states and starts to help Andy off the stool.

"Wait, we need to finish our regular drink now," Julia protests, and this causes the guys to groan in frustration.

"I got one that we can do and finish off our drink," Len says from across the table. I look at her, and she smiles. She picks up her phone and types away on it. A few seconds later, my phone lights up. I see what she typed up, and my lips tip up knowing this is going to kill Neil to hear.

"Okay, last one, I promise." We raise our glasses that are about half full. I turn and stare straight into Neil's eyes. "Here's to all of the men we've had, some were good, some were bad, some will run, some will follow, but it's up to us if we spit or swallow."

I toss back my glass, downing the rest of it, and go to put it back on the table. The glass doesn't even make it halfway from my lips before it's out of my hands and I'm flying over his shoulder. Glancing over at Len, I see her laughing.

Yep, I knew him hearing me talk about other men would do the trick. I will need to thank her for that.

NEIL

Watching Sara have her fun tonight brought a smile to my face. At first, I didn't want her out of the house. But after seeing her face when I said I wasn't sure, I knew I needed to cave. I couldn't keep her from her girls. She needed to get out of the house, and since the guys all said they would help guard and, well, I would do anything for her.

Currently, we are about halfway back to the house. She drove me crazy with her toasts of pussy, cock, and orgasms. That last one, hearing her talk of other men? Yeah, that was the last straw. I stormed to her little ass and threw her over my shoulder with the thought that I would show her just who was in charge of if she spits or swallows.

The bedroom is my domain, and she knows this. She's a very independent person, and I never want to take away her spirit or her independence, but I'll be the one to take control and allow her to have that moment where she won't have to think about what will come next. Even if it's only during sex that I take those choices from her. With that one toast, I knew she was challenging me. Actually, I knew after the second toast she was telling me she's done with me holding back.

I know the doctor gave the all-clear, but I couldn't stop myself from walking away each time I saw the bruises. What she doesn't understand is that no matter what, her health comes first. Blue balls suck, but I refuse to hurt her or take her before she's fully healed. The thought of her being in pain, and not in a good way, has me praying she will knock out in the truck on the drive back to the house.

As I pull up to our gate I hear a soft snore beside me. *Thank God.*

It takes me about thirty minutes to get her up to our room and into bed. Staring down at her, I quickly undress and climb up beside her. She turns in her sleep and cuddles up against me. I smirk down at her head and kiss her hair. Just as I'm falling asleep, I hear her murmur, "Morning . . . you're mine."

Fuck me.

I'm in heaven.

That's all I can think of as I slowly come out of my sleepy haze. The sheet that's covering me is moving and I glance over at the clock. It's only four in the morning. We've been asleep for maybe four hours. I turn back to the site of the sheet moving, and try my hardest not to let her know that

I'm awake. However, after a few moments I feel myself hit the back of her throat, and that does it.

I fling the fucking cover off me and see the sexiest sight I've ever had the pleasure of seeing. Sara's soft pink lips are wrapped around my cock, and she has her right hand wrapped around the part that she can't reach. I follow the line of her left arm and see she's playing with herself as she's sucking me off.

"Fuck, Sara. How wet are you, *Habibti*? Give me your hand."

At my command, she pulls her hand away from herself and slowly brings it to my lips. Grabbing her wrist, I stare right into her eyes as I suck her fingers into my mouth. The sweet tangy taste that's all Sara bursts on my tongue and has me moaning and closing my eyes. Fuck, I can't take it anymore.

Before I cum into her mouth, I reach down, grab her hair, and pull her mouth off me.

"Get your pussy up here. One taste isn't going to do," I growled out at her as I pull her on top of me, making her straddle my face.

I grab her ass and then dive in. Jesus, I can't get enough of her taste. The need of having her on my lips and tongue is enough to drive me mad. My fingers squeeze her cheeks even harder, and I know I'm leaving bruises. Those I'm fine with. Those are my marks. Those will remind her that I'm in charge of her orgasms.

It doesn't take but a few moments before she's screaming out my name with her body shaking in the throes of her crashing over the edge. I gently slow my licks and sucks to prolong her orgasm for as long as I can. Once she starts to slump down, I slide her down my body and thrust up into her in one long, hard stroke. Damn, her tightness squeezes me to the point of pain. I know it won't be long before I'm emptying into her.

"Fuck. You're so damn tight."

"Neil," is whimpered out of her lips, which makes me look down at her as I wait for her body to adjust to my invasion.

"You okay, Sara?"

After a few deep breaths, she sits up and looks down at me with a small smirk, and it's then that I remember I was trying to hold off until the bruises were healed. The fucking minx knew what she was doing.

"*Habibti*."

"Who's in charge?"

That's it.

I quickly change positions, then look down at her face with my signature smirk. Slowly I raise her arms above her head, holding them in one hand as I quickly grab the tie and secure her wrists above her.

"What are you . . ." She looks up at her wrists then looks back at me.

"You'll learn quickly that I'm always in charge in the bedroom. Trust, Sara. It's about trust. Trust me to know just how much you can take. If, for some reason, it's too much, make sure you say slow or stop. We don't need safe words. *Stop* or *no* will always work, and we can reassess and then decide to continue or end it."

The look on her face has me holding my breath. I may not be into hardcore dom shit, but I do like my control. After a few moments, she nods her head. My heart swells more knowing she's trusting me this way.

Fuck, I'm sounding like a pussy.

My lips slam into hers, and I demand entrance past her lips. I slowly drag out of her wet velvet heat and then slam into her. Swallowing her moans, I continue to repeat the slow withdraw and fast, hard thrust back in. It isn't but minutes before I feel her starting to tighten into another orgasm.

Nope, I'm not ready for her to have another one. I quickly pull out and flip her onto her stomach, mindful that her arms are still bound.

"Damn it, Neil," she screams in protest and gives me a look as if she's trying to kill me with her eyes.

My hand raises, and I give her a look back, telling her to watch herself. She narrows her eyes at me, daring me to even try it. As my hand slaps her ass, I thrust hard back into her. She throws her head back, moaning loudly, and clenches around my cock. Fuck. Seeing my hand print forming on her ass has me slapping her other cheek. With each slap I give her, she clenches even more tightly around me and has me fighting the impending orgasm that's about to crash over my body.

"Fuck . . . so fucking tight . . . so fucking good. Mine, Sara. Do you understand? Mine! Say it," I growl at her as I start thrusting harder into her.

"Neil," she whimpers.

"No. You will not come until you tell me you're mine, *Habibti*. Now say it, or I'll stop."

She's too lost in her pleasure that she just moans, and that just isn't working for the caveman part of me. I thrust in deep and hard, then hold myself there.

"Please."

"Say it, Sara. Say you're mine."

"Yes. I'm yours, Neil. Now let me come," she grunts at me over her shoulder.

Hearing her say she's mine sends me into a frenzy and has me rutting into her harder and faster. I can tell she's on the edge and needs just a bit more to send her over. My hand raises and slaps her ass one more time. She screams her orgasm out as she pulses over my cock.

Lightning shoots down my spine, and I pump my cock into her two more times before I start to feel my body convulse with pleasure. After a few more thrusts, I fall over to my side and gently pull Sara with me. I untie her wrists, then slowly rub them, making sure I work the circulation back into her arms while I keep placing gentle kisses on her neck.

"You okay?" I ask.

She nods her head and then snuggles up against me.

"Ahebbouka aktar men ayga, Habibti." I start dozing off and then I barely hear in a soft voice.

"Ahebbouka aktar men ayga, Habibi."

Twenty

Sara

MY ATTENTION ISN'T ON WHAT it should be, which is filing paperwork into the company computer system. No, my attention is on the soreness that's going on between my legs. It has been three days since girls' night, and I'm still sore. At least my ass isn't stinging when I sit anymore. The bruises from his fingers are still there but slowly fading. I feel myself growing wet at the thought of him taking control again. He took me again in the morning when he questioned me on how I knew to call him *Habibi*. Once I told him I wanted to know what a woman calls her man in Arabic, he growled, and attacked again demanding me to repeat it over and over.

We haven't had a chance for an encore because there was some talk that Diego and his crew were sniffing around. At the thought of that, my arousal dies quickly. I'm worried because I know they will do anything to find me and end my life so there would be no witnesses. The dread of them hurting someone close to me again washes over me and has me panicking.

Standing up, I walk over to the window to try to calm down and pull my thoughts away from the bad. I keep telling myself that I'm safe here. They can't get to me. Neil and the boys will protect me and those I love. I trust them.

The color red catches my eye, and I glance over to see what it is. My breath catches when I see it's my journal. Taking the few steps over to it, I pick it up and flip through the pages. The built-in bookmark is on the entry where I called myself his Habibti. My eyes close at the thought that I'm putting everyone I love in harm, and I again start to think that maybe I should call Conti and see if he can come get me to a safe house.

The journal makes me think about my name.

Who really am I? Rebecca or Sara?

I kept this journal to keep myself aware that Rebecca is really who I am. However, over the years I became a new person. I became more independent and more mature. I'm not sure if I'm Rebecca anymore. I know at some point I'm going to have to decide who I am and which name I'm going to keep. Sara was my mom's middle name, and Reyes was the last name of one of my favorite authors. That's why I picked it. But part of me feels that by not keeping the name Rebecca, I'm washing away the memory of my parents who loved me with everything they were.

The ringing of the phone snaps me out of my thoughts. Rushing over to my desk, I pick up my phone and don't recognize the number that's displaying. It has to be the office calls that are sent to my phone.

"Seal Security." Nobody says anything, so I try again. "Seal Security, Sara speaking."

"You aren't really Sara, though, are you?" A voice I

somewhat recognize speaks on the other line.

"I'm sorry?" Chuckling comes through the phone, and the hairs on the back of my neck start to stand.

"Tsk-tsk, Rebecca. You can't fool me. Just letting you know that you aren't as safe as you think you are," Diego murmurs.

Stunned, I just sit there, saying nothing.

"Nice blue sundress. Love it. Can't wait to see it off you before I kill you. They can't keep you safe much longer. I don't understand why you just don't give up, Rebecca . . . or should I say, Sara?" he asks, sighing out my name. "See you soon."

The line goes dead, and I just sit there shaking. I glance down at my dress and wonder how he knows.

God, I'm not as safe as I thought.

A ping from my phone has me looking down at it, and my hand starts shaking, seeing it's a text from an unknown number. A scream fills the room at what I see. There's a picture of me that was taken a few moments ago, when I was standing at the window. There's a target right at my forehead. It was taken through a scope of a gun. The second picture is one of Neil who is in the kitchen making us lunch with a target on the back of his head. The message attached states, "**Again, not very safe are you. Bye for now.**"

Before I realize it, Neil's by my side and holding me, trying to calm me down. Thoughts of him getting hurt because of me run through my mind, and I know I'm going to have to do something that he might never forgive me for.

I'm going to have to run.

Again.

NEIL

It has been a day from hell already. I'm so ready for it to be bedtime that I'm tempted to pull Sara out of the office and to bed after we eat lunch. The past three days, the boys and I've been working with Conti trying to pin down where Diego is at. There was chatter that got back to us that he's searching for her. The sooner we can find him and his men, the faster I can tie Sara to me completely.

I rub the front of my jeans, feeling the ring that's sitting in my pocket. A few days after she ran, I went and ordered her engagement ring. It's a three-carat princess-cut diamond ring that has two smaller round diamonds on each side. The wedding band has baguette diamonds that goes halfway around it. It's set in fourteen-karat white gold.

After Dante reminded me of the Arabic saying, I then took it back to the jeweler and had him engrave it on the inside of both rings. After that I went and got her name tattooed over my heart with the saying under it. She finally saw it after she woke up from her nap the day she came home. The tears that she cried tore my heart apart, until she told me they were happy tears. I can handle a lot of things, but her crying isn't one of them. Those damn tears would make me do anything to make them stop. I just pray she never figures that shit out.

Screams coming from the office stop my thoughts. I can feel the fear in her scream, and it has me dropping everything and running to her. When I reach her, I scoop her up and start trying to calm her down. She's shaking and her face is pale while she stares down at the phone in her hand. I glance down, and what I see on her phone has my muscles pulling tight and me seeing red. Reminding myself that I'm holding her, I take a few deep breaths, then slowly take the phone from her. I need to get her to calm down, and then I can deal with this shit.

"Sara, breathe. Deep breaths in and out. There you go, *Habibti*. That's it. Now, let's go upstairs and relax while the boys take care of this, okay?"

At her nod, I quickly send a text to Ghost telling him to get the boys over here and to look through her phone that's on her desk. Then I take her upstairs, crawl into bed with her, and hold her close to my body, softly telling her it will be okay and that we'll get to the bottom of everything. It's about forty minutes later before I feel her completely relax, letting me know she finally fell asleep. Gently kissing her forehead, I get out of bed, trying not to wake her.

Docs head snaps up at the sound of me entering the office.

"How in the fuck did that piece of shit get those pictures?"

"There was also a call that lasted for a few minutes. You're not going to be happy when you hear it," Sin murmurs from the phone. He's still in Piersville.

Doc hits play, and I can't help the rage that runs through my veins. The thought of murder runs through my mind, and my vision starts to go through a tunnel. All I can see is Diego at the end of my gun and I'm emptying my magazine into his chest.

"*Habibi*, please come back to me," is barely making its

way into my mind as the feel of familiar hands is rubbing down my back. It takes me a few moments to focus and come out of my dark thoughts I'm having.

The room is destroyed, and I realize that I'm in a bear hug against Eagle.

Fuck!

I haven't had this type of reaction since Len was taken. Nobody but Eagle knows about that episode. After a few deep breaths, I give Eagle a nod, letting him know that I'm good again, then slowly turn toward Sara and pull her into my arms. She's shaking, and her face is pale with worry.

"Sara, I'm fine, *Habibti*. Sorry to scare you."

"I heard a loud noise, like someone roaring, then I heard the crashing of things being thrown. What happened?"

"Nothing you need to worry about right now. Why don't we phone the girls and have you all stay in the basement tonight? This way the guys and I can get to the bottom of the call and text." At the mention of the word 'call' she goes stiff in my arms.

"You know about that?" is barely whispered out of her beautiful mouth.

"Yeah, we tapped your lines. Need to make sure you're safe. Go ahead and call them. Doc, call the parents, Ghost, Conti, and Winters. Have them come. Tell them to plan to stay the night."

We need to get a plan together to keep her safe. It will be a long night, but it doesn't matter. Sara's safety is worth it. She's about ready to see the beast mode that I keep hidden. Nobody threatens the woman that means more than anything to me.

Sara

"Sara, I know what you're thinking and it isn't going to work." Ashley is standing there with her arms crossed and is tapping her foot at me. "He'll just come after you."

"What are you talking about, Ashley?" Confusion is etched on everyone's face as they try to figure out what she's saying to me.

"She's thinking of running."

"Sara, you can't run!" Len throwing her hands in the air in exasperation.

"Wait . . . why don't you tell us what happened. You never told us why you're in witness protection, and the boys aren't talking." Julia walks back in from the small kitchen that's off to the right with a tray of drinks in her hand.

"First, please don't shout. OPG, Pops, Papa Tony, Momma Connie, and Momma Gio all went upstairs to bed and I don't need Neil running down here demanding to know why I'm thinking of running." Standing, I start pacing in the small living room.

"This is a safe room, Sara. So he isn't going to hear since the door is shut," Winters explains.

"What do you mean *safe room*?" Julia looks over at her, waiting for an explanation.

They all listen as she explains what the meaning is. I have to give it to Neil; the design is nice. It's like it is its own little apartment or mother-in-law unit. There are three bedrooms on the east side of the basement, one slightly bigger than the other two, all done up simply in greens and blues. The one that's bigger has a full bath attached to it and the other full bath is between the other two. To the west is a game room of sorts. It has a pool table, dart board, and a table for poker. The center of the basement has the living room, kitchen, and dining room. Other than the bedrooms, it's an open floor plan and you can see everywhere. Along the wall in the living room is a huge TV with monitors off to the left of it and a huge bookcase to the right. The word *soundproof* catches my attention and brings me back to the discussion.

"So, there's no way the rambling stain dictator's upstairs can hear us? Oh, I demand girl talk in here from now on." Andy claps his hand thinking his idea is brilliant. I don't bother to tell him I'm sure Neil has it bugged.

"Andy, what did I tell you about that fucking application. I thought I blocked it from your phone!" Chris throws his hands up.

"I found a way around it. I can't have you messing up my nickname generator. The guys' love it deep down." Andy props his hands on his hips arching his eyebrow at his husband.

"I'm going to head to bed. I'm tired and have to get up early tomorrow for work." Chris stands and gives Andy a kiss goodnight then murmurs, "Don't be long. I love you."

"Love you too, doctor sexy ass." Andy slaps Chris on the ass as he walks away and we all tell him goodnight.

"That's so sweet. Now, this safe room stuff . . . I think Dante should have one built in our home." Everyone is nodding their heads.

"Okay, back at the subject at hand. Sara, start talking." Andy plops down in the spot I was sitting in.

After a lot of tears, cussing, and comfort from everyone, I finally got through my story. The only one who was somewhat silent was Winters because she knew the story. However, I still saw tears flowing down here face when I got to the part of what I heard the EMT say about Arturo's heartbeat.

"Dear God. I can't even imagine." Andy's holding his chest, shaking his head.

Looking around the room, I notice that they all have looks of disbelief, heartache, and something else that I'm now realizing is pity. That's the one feeling I can't take from people. I don't want people to pity me. Anger starts to boil in my veins and I can feel my control starting to snap.

"Don't! Just, fucking don't! I don't want nor need your damn pity. Yeah, the situation is fucked up, and I've been through hell. But I'm a strong person. This is one of the reasons I never wanted you all to know. Save your pity for someone else." I turn and stomp to one of the bedrooms and slam the door.

Fifteen minutes later, the door cracks open and footsteps sound. I'm sitting on the side of the bed and staring at some picture on the wall which I still can't tell you what it is.

"Sara . . . I don't think they were giving you pity. I think they were hurting because they love you and are scared for you. I know this is hard and that dealing with this is a lot to battle with daily, but I think you need to realize that you're a survivor. Also, not many have met someone who has been through what you went through and come out on the other side so strong. I have a feeling some of the looks you were seeing is admiration and awe at the strength you have."

Winters sits down beside me.

"She's right . . . I look at you like a hero. I wish I had your strength." Ashley's voice floats in from behind me.

Before I realize it, the bed's crowded with everyone climbing on it behind me.

"That's the thing. I'm not strong. I'm so freaking weak inside. I put on a show for everyone on the outside. You all might think I have it all figured out . . . but I don't even know who I am anymore," I sob.

"What do you mean?" Julia asks.

"I don't know who I am anymore," I repeat. "I was born Rebecca, but ten years ago, I became Sara. I wrote in my journal as Rebecca so I wouldn't forget who I was. Part of me feels guilty for thinking I'm no longer that person. Like I'm forgetting the memory of my parents by saying I'm no longer her. I've grown and changed so much. I had to change who I was to the person I am now, and I don't feel like Rebecca is part of me anymore."

"Well, according to the law you're Sara, not Rebecca. Right?" Ashley cocks her head at me.

"Actually, once this is over Sara will have to choose to keep the name she has or go back to her given name," Winters murmurs out. "Something she's going to have to think about."

"Well, there's time for that once it's over. You don't have to make that choice right now. And we are here to help you think it through. Now let's change this subject and talk about what happened after the bar when that sexy hunk of a man carried you out." Andy wiggles his eyebrows at me.

Chuckling, I snuggle down on the bed and start talking about the other night.

NEIL

We've been at it for hours and still haven't come up with a plan that would be good enough to get these fuckers. After the family came, we ate dinner and then got the woman settled downstairs. Winters wanted to be up here with us, but we wanted her to be with the girls. She's fully healed from the explosion, and I know that she's vital to the case. But I felt more comfortable with having one of us down there with the women. Plus, FBI Agent Weil convinced her to stay down there.

"There's only one thing that will get this over with and quick. We just need to make sure we control the situation," Sin's voice comes through the phone.

"I'm not going to say this again, so get it through your fucking heads. She will not be used as fucking bait!" I swear to God I'm going to kill these fucking people.

"Lucky, listen . . ." Conti starts, but then shuts his mouth quickly when I look at him. He wasn't here during my "episode" but he was filled in quickly. The one thing that shocked all of us is that Sara's voice and touch dragged me out of my mind faster than anyone has ever done before.

"Can I give an idea?" Winters's voice sounds behind me. "They all knocked out, so I decided to come up here and see if I can be of any help."

"B, I think . . ." Weil started to speak, but Sin interrupted him.

"Let's hear it."

"I know you don't want to put her in jeopardy. But I

think there might a solution and it's something you can control. There's a book signing in downtown Kansas City that has a lot of authors Sara loves. I was able to score ten VIP tickets for the weekend. Don't tell the girls, but we can set it up with the coordinator and the hotel to allow you all in. This leaves her in public but in a large crowd, which is going to be a good thing. Diego isn't going to make a big scene to bring attention to the cartel. So, he'll try to get her alone and out the door. But with us surrounding the building, he won't have a chance to do anything."

The room is silent as we process what she just said. I hate to admit it, but she's right. If we can get it worked out, then it would be a way to handle the situation.

"Why not tell the girls what's going on? Them knowing might help them stay vigilant and look out for each other," Conti asks.

"Actually, they might put more of a show on if they know. We need them to act as natural as possible. Draws less attention. Good thinking, B." Weil stands and walks over to Winters, pressing a soft kiss on her forehead.

Everyone turns to look at me, and I know they're waiting to see if I'm game for this. I look over at Pops to see what he thinks. He always has a way of seeing things from a logical point, and I trust his gut just as much as I trust mine. After a few moments of staring at each other, he gives a small nod.

"All right, let's get the details all worked out before they wake up."

Twenty-One

NEIL

THE SUN'S SLOWLY STARTING TO rise off in the distance, and I know I'm going to have to wake Sara up soon. Today is the day of the signing, and we were able to get a plan in place. The women, other than Winters, have no clue what's going to hopefully go down. We placed some chatter out in the community with the right people that they were going to a signing downtown. Hoping it will get to Diego and his crew so we can finally end this shit.

Glancing at the clock, I see we have about thirty minutes before I have to wake her up. A smirk starts to form on my lips at the best way to wake my woman up; I'm going to return the favor she did for me the other day.

As gently as I could, I slowly start to remove the blanket and sheet off her body. Turning her onto her back was easier than I figured it would be. Her already being naked is a bonus. It wasn't hard to talk her into coming to bed nude after I showed her the other night just how beneficial it would be.

God, her curves drive me crazy. Her skin is smooth and is begging me to lick it slowly. So, I decide that's exactly what I'm going to do. Starting with those perky tits with those peach-colored nipples that get hard enough to cut diamonds once my mouth touches them.

I wrap my lips gently around her left nipple and slowly flick my tongue over it. After a few moments, I start kissing over to her right nipple giving it the same attention, then start to make my way down her body.

Watching her face, I slowly make my way between her gorgeous legs and place my arms under them. I'm so fucking hard, and I have precum leaking out onto the sheets. I can smell her wetness that's slowly starting to form on her pussy lips. My mouth starts watering. My need to taste her overwhelms me, and I take a swipe at her pussy lips. The tastes floods my tongue, and it's the most delicious thing I've ever tasted. I'm so addicted to her flavor.

Lick after lick and nip after nip, I finally get a moan out of my girl. She was sleeping deeply. I go a little harder at her clit and decide to add my fingers into the mix. Just as I enter two into her, I feel her hands dig into my hair and my name slip from her lips.

"Mmmm, good morning, *Habibti*. Thank you for my breakfast," I murmur against her pussy and then start really going to town. I need to fuck—no, not fuck—make slow, gentle love to her. I want her to see the soft side to my dominant side.

She detonates after a few more thrusts of my fingers, and I can't take it anymore. Quickly, I make my way up her body and thrust into her tight wet pussy. I can still feel her pulsing from her orgasm, and it causes me to slowly start thrusting into her.

"God, Neil, so good. Faster."

"Fuck, Sara. Your pussy owns me," I moan out, then take her lips and give her a deep, soul-shattering kiss. "This morning, I'm taking you slowly."

Over and over I slip into her heat while staring into her beautiful green eyes. Eyes that are telling me without words just how I affect her. Eyes that are screaming love that's so deep that I can't even begin to comprehend. I try to convey the same emotions with each thrust and each breath I take. Tears start to form in her eyes, and I hold her head between my hands as she wraps her arms around my neck.

Before I'm ready for it, I feel her start to tighten with her upcoming orgasm. This causes me to thrust slightly faster and harder. The need to see her shatter while I stare into her eyes is strong, and I start to feel the lightning slowly working its way up my spine. For some reason, this time feels different. I know I'm about to have the best orgasm of my life, and I pray it's the same for her.

"Neil . . ." she moans and starts to close her eyes.

"Open those beautiful eyes, Sara. I need to watch your eyes while you come."

Her lids snap open at my command, and four thrusts later, she starts convulsing around my cock and I can't hold back anymore.

"Ahebbouka aktar men ayga, Habibti," I softly murmur as I burst deep inside her, watching the emotions swirl all over her beautiful face.

I was right. This time was so much more different. More meaningful. More powerful. More soul shattering. Just more of everything, period.

"Ahebbouka aktar men ayga, Habibi."

I roll onto my back, taking her with me, and just hold her close to me. I say a quick prayer that today will go smoothly and then we can finally move on with the rest of our lives.

Sara

We're currently walking around the signing I'd been dying to go to. Well, before I had to go to the safe house, anyway. I'm not sure how Winters pulled it off, but she did. Glancing around, I can't help but smile as I see all the tables lined up with some of my favorite authors.

"Where to first?" Winters asks.

"Umm . . . I don't know. Let's just start to the left and make our way around. I want to end on seeing . . ." I start to say, but I'm cut off by someone.

"Brit . . . Over here!"

"Crystal!" Winters starts walking toward the woman who is yelling at us with her arms in the air. Looking at Andy and the girls, I shrug my shoulders and follow.

"I'm so glad you could make it. I want you to meet someone. Brit, this is a good friend of mine, Reggie. Reggie, this is my best friend from high school, Brittany Winters. She's a detective. Asshole is a photographer, 'R plus M Photos' is his photography name."

"You call him asshole?" I can't help but ask.

"Yep, it's a mutual understanding that it's a term of

endearment. Even his wife, Melissa, agrees with me."

"Those two are really the only ones who call me that. Most call me Panda. Nice to meet you as well."

Winters quickly makes introductions, and then we chat about the models we like that are on covers we have read. I'm shocked to find out that he has taken a few of them for the authors.

"That reminds me. Sara found a pretty hot model on her night out last week. She sent me a picture. I'll send it to you later, Crystal."

"Hey, Ah Panda, do you take family pictures?" Len asks with her hand on her stomach.

"Not really. I can, but I prefer to do bodybuilding and sport photography. However, my wife Melissa does. Her website is called 'Hey Beautiful.' Wait . . . what does Ah Panda mean?"

"Asshole Panda. I thought it was more appropriate," she tells him with a straight face, and this has Crystal clapping her hands in excitement.

"Fuck yes! Ah Panda. I love it."

"Do you have any prints on hand, Ah Panda?" Len asks, heading to the table behind him.

"Oh, hot men—hell yeah, I'm in!" Andy pipes up behind her.

Deciding I wanted books more than images, I make my way over to the first table. After about thirty minutes of talking to an author I never heard of, I look over and see they're still looking at images. Well, fuck it. I grab my phone and text Len that I'm running to the restroom really quick and will meet them at the next table.

The hotel restroom, that's across from the conference

room where the signing is being held, is actually pretty big. There are about sixteen stalls, eight on each side, two areas to wash your hands and two doors that have a seating area right by them. Each door leads to a hallway in the hotel. It seems empty, which I'm happy about because I don't like public restrooms.

After I right my clothes again after using the toilet, I exit the stall and see someone standing off to the side by the door I didn't come in. I start to walk the opposite way when I hear footsteps behind me. Glancing behind me, I see a sight that I didn't want to see again. The door opens behind him, but I don't dare take my eyes off of him.

"Rebecca, we meet again." Diego gives me a smug grin and raises his hand that has a gun in it. I know this is it—this is the end, and I'm just grateful nobody came into the bathroom with me.

I just stand there silently staring at him, waiting for him to reply with something. His two guys walk up and stand next to him, looking at me like they want to do the worst things they could think of to me.

"Here's what we're going to do, Rebecca. You're going to walk out the door with us, and we're going to go out the service entrance. You're not to make a sound, or I will have one of the guys here make the call to another associate of mine that's watching your friend's little boy . . . Marcus is his name, correct?" At the sound of his name, I start to shake and feel the blood drain from my face. "Judging by your reaction, I would guess that I got that correct. Now, I will have him go ahead and make sure Marcus visits Arturo in heaven, and that would just tear your man's family apart now, wouldn't it?"

I swallow against the burn in the back of my throat and take a deep breath to fight off the tears that want to start falling down my face. I refuse to give him the satisfaction of knowing that he's getting to me emotionally. He may hold the cards right now, but if I ever have a chance to get out of this, I'm going to have to keep my cool.

"I'll come with you."

"Excellent choice; not like you had one to begin with. Let's get going. Time is money," Diego states, and the two goons take a step toward me.

The door behind me starts to open, and I start to panic at what they're going to do to some innocent person who is walking in.

"Sara, what the heck? You're taking your . . ." Len stops mid-sentence as I spin and see she's taken in the situation. "Oh, God, no. Sara?"

"Len, go back outside. Pretend . . ." is all I can get out before I'm jerked back by one of the goons.

"Shut up. She's coming with us. No witnesses. It just looks like our lucky day, boys. We got two women to have fun with today."

"Please, she's almost eight months pregnant with twins. I swear she won't say anything. Please let her go. I already said I'll go with you." I'll do anything to protect Len and those babies. There's no way I could ever forgive myself if something happens to them because of me.

"No can do. She comes with us now, or I take her life here. So, what do you pick, Mrs. De Luca?" Diego asks her as he raises his gun her way.

"I'll go." She's looking at me in the eyes, and I can tell she's trying to convey something to me.

183

We all head out the other door and quickly make our way down to the service entrance. Right outside the door is a black SUV that has very dark, tinted windows.

"Phones, ladies," Goon One demands, holding out his hands.

Reaching into my back pocket, I pull out my phone and hand it to him. He takes a moment and holds his hand out toward Len, too.

"Does it look like I have a phone? I'm in sundress and sandals. There are no pockets," she huffs out and holds her arms out to her side

"Pat her down," Diego demands.

After a brisk pat down and them not finding anything, I silently watch as they smash my phone onto the concrete. We are then shoved into the back of the SUV and they start tying our hands with zip ties as we pull away from the hotel.

"Sit back and enjoy the ride, ladies. It's the last one you will ever get to experience. Well, alive, anyway."

Looking over at Len, I mouth, "I'm sorry," at her, and I have tears in my eyes. However, she has a small smile on her face and looks down at her wedding ring. I follow her line of sight and am puzzled at why she's smiling at her ring. Does she think that's going to stop them from raping or killing us?

She glances at me, then the ring again, and I honestly am not getting whatever message she's trying to send to me. As the SUV takes a sharp left heading into the area in Kansas City that has abandoned warehouses that they use to make into haunted houses during Halloween, Len leans into me, acting as if she's off balance. When she gets close enough to my ear, she barely whispers out, "Ring has tracker."

Helping her right herself, I try to keep the shock off my

face that Dante would put a tracker in her ring. Then again, it isn't that far off for him to do. He's obsessed with her, and after her kidnapping last year . . . yeah, I can totally see it.

"You okay?" I ask her once she's situated again.

"No talking!" Diego barks from the front.

"I was making sure she was okay after your goon decided to take that turn too fast and she fell into me. It won't happen again."

Out of the corner of my eye, I see her look down at her ring again. Maybe, just maybe, we will get out of this alive.

Twenty-Two

Sara

WE SLOWLY PULL INTO AN empty warehouse in downtown Kansas City. This puts me on edge and makes me cringe, knowing there isn't a lot of people around this area. Mostly druggies or criminals. There are times I wish the city would just tear these buildings down, but it holds so much history it would be a shame to lose them. Plus, they do make for some amazing haunted houses.

A bay door starts to open and I hold my breath, hoping that Len's tracker will still work.

"Take them to the back room and lock them in there. I have an idea, and I need to talk to Roman first."

"Sure, boss. Tray, let's have some fun." Goon One smiles back at us with a look that I'm not liking.

"Willie, no fun yet. I don't want them hurt. Just take them in the room like I said. If I find one mark on them, I will not hesitate to do to you what you did to them," Diego states and exits the SUV.

"Guess you *putas* are safe for the time being. Let's go,"

Tray says, not looking happy about the orders given.

Len goes to step out but stops and her breath catches in her throat.

"Len?"

"Shit. Not now, damn it!" Len grunts out and she grabs her stomach as best as she can.

"What the fuck? Let's go, we don't have time for your bullshit," Willie speaks out harshly.

After a few deep breaths, Len continues out of the SUV, and I follow quickly. We're taken to a room that's full of dust and old rusty tables that line the walls. I take a quick look around and try to see if there's anything that we could use to defend ourselves. They quickly undo the zip ties before walking toward the exit.

"Don't get any ideas. This room is clean of weapons. Get comfy—it might be a few hours before our guest of honor is going to be here," Diego pipes up from the doorway before Trey and Willie walk out of it. With a sinister smile, he shuts the door and we hear a lock engage.

"Who do you think he's talking about?" Len murmurs, then takes a seat on the floor.

"Don't know . . ." I trail off because I notice she has a tightened look on her face. "Len, what's wrong?"

"I think I'm in labor. I've been having pains all day, thinking they're just Braxton Hicks, but they're getting stronger."

"And you didn't think of mentioning this earlier? Wait . . . isn't it too early? You're only eight months pregnant!"

"First, I wanted to go to the signing, so I thought I would have time if it was active labor. Secondly, twins are normally delivered early. I'm okay right now . . . they're about fifteen minutes apart. I'm just trying to relax, and hopefully that will calm them down. If anything, remember I'm a doctor. I just don't want to have them in here if I can help it."

I rush by her side, sit down, and then guide her to lay her head into my lap.

"Relax and rest as much as you can. Let's just pray the guys can still track us," I tell her while gently brushing her hair away from her face. "I'm sorry, Len."

"Hush . . . this isn't your fault, Sara. I love you and honestly, I'm glad I walked in when I did. However, I'm beginning to second guess public bathrooms and me."

"Oh, God, you're right. What is it with you and public restrooms and being kidnapped? Dante will definitely ban them in the future." I start chuckling at the thought. "I love you, too. Now, rest."

I say a quick prayer, hoping that they will realize quickly we are missing and not just running from table to table meeting authors.

It's been about an hour and Len's contractions are getting stronger and closer together. I'm afraid I'm going to have to deliver these twins myself. The longer we're here, the more I'm afraid the guys aren't going to be able to find us.

The sound of the bay door opening again has me cringing. I have a feeling that whoever it is, it isn't the help that I've been so desperately praying for.

"You doing okay?"

"Just getting tired and uncomfortable. I should walk around, but I don't want to bring on the labor any faster."

Len gently sits up and stretches a bit.

"Maybe a few laps around this room might help just stretch you out a bit. If you start to feel it's beginning to bring it on faster, we can stop and rest again." I'm hoping she says yes because my ass is numb from sitting on the floor for so long.

Before she can answer, we hear voices and steps coming closer to the door. We glance at each other before I quickly stand and help her to her feet.

Tray and Willie appear in the doorway and are smiling at us.

"Well, ladies, it's time for you to learn about one of your futures."

"What do you mean 'one of our futures'?" Len questions Willie.

"Well, one of you will bring us a lot . . ." Tray starts off but is quickly cutoff by a slap to the back of his head when Diego walks into the room. I spot someone behind him, but he's too far back for me to make out anything.

"Shut your fucking mouth. Now, Rebecca and Len, I have a nice surprise for you. See, I was thinking on the drive here, and I had a brilliant idea. After talking to my good friend, Roman, he agreed with my brilliant idea and is here to pick one of you up."

Len starts to tighten up again from a contraction and squeezes my hand hard. This catches Diego's eye.

"What's wrong with her?"

I glance at Len and she gives me a look like she doesn't want me to say anything. But maybe, just maybe, the guy behind them will help.

"She's in labor," I murmur out, still holding her gaze,

hoping she understands why I told them.

"Oh goodie. With her being a doctor, that makes this process much easier. I would like for you to meet your babies and your fate, Len. Please meet my good friend, Roman. He buys and sells women."

My stomach drops at the last sentence that came out of Diego's mouth, and I turn my head toward the door and watch as Diego, Tray, and Willie all step away from the door to make room for the newcomer.

"Hello, ladies."

The guy who walks into the room isn't someone I was expecting to see as an associate of Diego's. There's no way this is real. A small smirk forms on his face, and I know that it's real and I lose all hope of getting out of here alive.

NEIL

Thirty minutes earlier . . .

Glancing around the room, I take in the people who are here to help make this work. We have all our guys except Sin, however he's on the phone and working with Mace and Coleman in Piersville. Even the twins came in from Italy to help out. Conti has some of his guys here, and Weil brought in some feds to help as well. I'm still a little uneasy, but I'm glad we have so many people here.

We placed some undercover men to keep an eye on the entrances and a few also roaming in the signing room. We dropped Andy, the moms, OPG, the girls, and the dads off about thirty minutes ago. I'm glad the dads are with them since they know what is going on, but I'm now second guessing not telling the rest of them. They think we are heading to Crown Center to take in a movie while they're here at the hotel.

"Are you sure it's a good idea to keep them in the dark?" I ask Weil as I take a seat next to him.

"Trust me, they need to act as natural as possible."

"What's your name, by the way?" Doc asks, turning toward us.

"Curt. Now that you know that, explain the nicknames."

"Seal call signs. Well, Ghost, whose real name is Dante, is because he can enter a building or room that's full of people and nobody knows he's even there until it's too late. Eagle, or Justice, is a sniper. Our eyes in the sky. Sin, also known as John, is something that just stuck. The asshole is the one who got all the girls and they kept saying 'he was sexy as sin.' I'm called Doc, or James, because I was a corpsman and have medical training. And Neil, aka Lucky, is because that asshole is one lucky son of a bitch when it came to missions. Thing One and Thing Two, Carlo and Nicoli is named that because that's what Ghost calls them," Doc explains while watching Weil's face.

"Why did you all leave the Seals?" an agent asks.

I look over toward Doc and see him stiffen. We try not to think of the mission that ended up making the choice of walking away so easy for our team.

"Life is what happened. What's up with you and Winters?" Eagle asks from across the room.

"It's a long story, but honestly she's more like a baby sister to me. We were on a case together a few years ago," he explains with a smirk on his face. "At first, I wanted something with her, however, she ended up falling for someone that was also involved in the case."

"She said she wasn't with anyone when the girls asked her," Nicoli states.

"Yes. Something happened, and they aren't together anymore. So, I'm protective of her like Conti is with Sara."

"Seems like there's a lot more to the story," Conti murmurs.

"There is, but that's for another day."

"Who wants coffee?" Eagle pipes up from the door with Ghost following behind him.

While we are all getting our coffee they got for us, I can't help but notice that Ghost is silent and glaring at his phone. Before I can ask him what is wrong, there's a phone ringing in the background.

"Excuse me for a moment . . . I need to take this," Weil states before making his way out of the room.

"Neil. I have a bad feeling about this. Len and Sara's names are turning my gut, and I think we need to tell them we are here. I've been trying to get ahold of Len on text, and she hasn't answered," Ghost says while still looking at his phone.

"You and your fucking gut feelings." Nicoli stands then walks over to Eagle.

"Eagle, check the monitors and see if they're all in the room still. Ghost, have you texted one of the dads?" Doc asks.

"Yeah, I just messaged Pops and am waiting to see what he says."

After a few moments, his phone pings and as he reads the message, I see his shoulders relax a bit.

"Pops says Len and Sara are in the bathroom."

Weil walks in and has a grim look on his face as he looks over at Ghost and me. A sense of dread begins to fill me before he even opens his mouth. "Diego has Len and Sara."

"Brother, let's get the intel first. We need to know what we are dealing with before we head down there." I hear from my left but can't make out the voice.

Before I realize it, I have him by his throat and up against the door. Eagle and Doc are trying to get me off him, and I hear a commotion behind me. I assume it's someone trying to contain Ghost from reaching him.

"What do you mean they have them? And how the fuck do you know this?" I growl between clenched teeth.

"Lucky, let him go so he can answer you, damn it!" Doc says to the left of me.

"If you kill him now you're not going to be any use in finding the girls. Now let him fucking go before I knock you on your ass," Eagle says into my ear.

I ease up on his throat, but I don't let him go and don't move from my position.

"That was a call from my boss telling me that I should be expecting a call. Let's take a seat. I have some things I need to fill you in on," he chokes out. "Neil, I'm undercover in the cartel. That's how I know so much. Now, let me the fuck go so I can finish telling you everything and we can work on a fucking plan."

His statement shocks me, and it's exactly what the boys need to drag me off of him.

"You're undercover with the cartel that has been after Sara for years? Did you not think to tell us this the other night when we were planning this whole operation?" I scream and try to lunge for him again.

"Lucky, fucking stop. Let's sit down and hear what he has to say. Then we need to figure out how to get our girls." Ghost's voice seems awfully calm.

"How can you be so calm?" I question.

"Because Len's wedding ring has a tracker on it. I know we can find them. I just need the intel on how many we're looking at. Eagle, can you pull up her location?" Ghost asks, then walks over to the couch and sits down.

I take a few deep breaths before jerking out of Doc and Eagle's hold.

"Talk," I demand to Weil as I take my seat next to Ghost.

"I can't go into many details other than I've been with them for close to two years now. That's why I was called out here to begin with. The higher-ups aren't happy with how Diego's handling things. Honestly, they never gave the order to go after Sara. Diego wasn't authorized to even do the crime he did years ago. He did it to see if he could move up the ladder. He seems to think that if he now eliminates the threat of Sara's testimony, it will make him look good and maybe move him up. What he doesn't understand is they aren't impressed and don't like killing women or children."

"So then why haven't they taken him out or told him to stop?" Sin asks from the speaker phone.

"They can't take him out because they're being watched. They know this, so they're trying their hardest to cover their tracks. Plus, the head of the cartel has been sick for a few years, and is on his deathbed. This will shake up everything, so they can't chance shit right now."

"Okay, so what does this have to do with us right now? We need to figure out how and what we are going to do to get them back. If he's that unstable and isn't listening to anyone that puts them in major jeopardy." Ghost stands up, and goes to the window to look out.

"That's why I'm expecting a call. They have a feeling they're going to want to try to sell Len because she's pregnant. And I'm the one they call for such things."

As if on cue, his phone rings and silence fills the room.

"Diego, what can I do for you?"

Whatever is said on the other line can't be good because it has Weil turning white and his lips pull into a thin white line.

Please, God, don't let us be too late.

Twenty-Three

Sara

I'M STILL IN SHOCK AT what I'm seeing.

"Oh, my God. You followed us that night, didn't you?" Len whispers.

"Smart girl," he chuckles out.

"Why?" is all I can manage to choke out.

"When Diego showed me a picture of you with your friends a few weeks ago, well, I knew I needed you for my collection," Roman, or Rome as we know him, says with a smile.

"You aren't gay, then?"

A booming laughter fills the room as he shakes his head at us.

"No, not even close to being gay."

"What are your plans for us?"

"There's no 'us,' Rebecca. Just Len," Diego states off from the side.

Rome slowly swings his head in his direction.

"Oh, no, my friend, I'm taking them both. This is an

order from the boss."

"No, that one is ours. We have unfinished business with her!" Willie roars, pointing directly at me.

Before I can even blink, there's a loud crack that fills the air. I watch in horror as Willie falls to the ground, not moving.

"Diego and Tray, any reason I need to keep you around?"

Turning to face Rome, I see both of them shake their heads and then run out the door. I can't take my eyes off of Rome. He's staring right at Len and me with a smile on his face.

"You killed him," Len whispers out.

"You're welcome." Oh, God, this guy is crazy to think we are grateful that he killed Willie.

"What are you going to do with us?" Len asks again.

Chuckling, he turns and starts heading toward the exit.

"I'll return with stuff so you can deliver the babies." And with that he closes and engages the lock again.

"Fuck, Sara, what are we going to do?" she asks while looking back over at Willie again.

"I don't know. But let's get you comfy again. I don't know how long it's going to be before he returns. I noticed you were trying hard not to let on that you were in a lot of pain. How far apart are they?"

"Seven minutes."

With a nod, I help her lay back down and say another quick prayer that this ends soon.

"Breathe, Len."

"Fuck, this shit hurts. I swear to fucking God if we get out of this, Dante's never getting his dick inside me again," she screams out through another contraction.

It has been about two hours since Rome has left us. Thirty minutes after they walked out, Diego and Tray came in and took Willie's body out. I heard talk that Rome had plans to sell Len and the babies first. Then they would talk about what would happen with me.

Len's water ended up breaking about an hour after, and now her contractions are about two minutes apart. There's nothing around us, and I'm not sure what to do. Even if Len keeps saying she can walk me through it.

"Len, you have done this before, and without drugs. Come on, you got this."

"Shut the fuck up, Sara. When you're in labor, I'll remind you of this moment."

If we get out of this, I would welcome it with open arms, I think to myself.

Diego and Rome walk in this time with some bags. I hold my breath, hoping that it's just items we might need to deliver the babies if we need to.

"Here you go, ladies."

"We need some hot distilled water, too," Len grunts through yet another contraction.

"Who are you selling them to?" I ask Rome.

"That isn't your business. Diego, go tell the others we need some hot water."

Diego quickly takes off to do his bidding. I still don't understand how Rome is a criminal. I would have never guessed he was part of the crime world.

"Why are you looking at me like that, *ninita*?"

"I just never thought you would be a criminal. You don't give off that vibe."

"You would be shocked to find out what I'm truly like," he murmurs, and something flashes across his face. "Enough about me. Let's get your friend here ready to meet her babies."

A loud bang sounds from outside, and I hear people shouting. Len looks up at me with worry etched on her beautiful face. Smiling, I try to convey that all is okay now.

"Where the fuck are they?" I hear Neil's voice clear as day, and that eases everything inside me.

"What the fuck are you doing here?" Tray screams.

"Where's my woman and sister?"

I go to open my mouth to scream, but the look on Rome's face stops me in my tracks.

"I wouldn't if I were you. Keep silent," he says while pulling a gun and pointing it toward Len's stomach.

"Please," I barely get the words out of my mouth.

"You got five seconds to answer me or I'm going to start putting bullets in your bodies," Neil shouts out.

Rome kneels beside me just as I hear gunshots ringing out in the warehouse. Instantly, I'm slammed again back to my past. I can't live through this again. No way can I live knowing Neil is now gone. The feelings that swamp me are so overwhelming that I can't handle it anymore. Blackness descends, and I barely make out the words that Rome says quietly to me . . .

"I'm not who you think I am."

After Weil took the phone call from Diego, we quickly started making a rescue plan. The part that sucks the most is that Weil can't come with us due to his cover. He ended up going and taking the family to Mom and Pops' house with the promise to keep them safe.

"ETA?" Ghost asks as we make our way to the warehouse they're at.

"Ten." Conti then picks up the phone and types out something on it. "I'm getting the swat together. We are wanting them alive. We know there are at least seven people there. We also know that Willie was killed."

I stretch my neck and get prepared for the breach into the warehouse.

"Are we sure we should go in loud?" I question.

"Yep, I know the cartel doesn't care what happens to the team. They would be grateful if the police would just kill them off." Weil speaks up from the phone in Conti's hand.

"Do we know where they're located at in the warehouse?" Doc asks.

"No idea. But I did just get word . . . be prepared–Len's in labor. I have an ambulance going in silent and will be down the street ready to pull in when you give me the all clear," Conti clips out

"FUCK!" Ghost screams.

Yeah, fuck is right. Len being in labor isn't something we needed right now.

"Get your buds in and let's test them before we pull up," Weil demands.

I look over at Ghost and see his grim expression. I know he's thinking of the last time Len was in labor.

"We'll make it, brother. Keep your head," I murmur, putting in my ear bud.

He says nothing as he puts his bud in.

"Okay, two minutes," cracks into my ear.

"Sounds good. I will go in first. Ghost and Doc, you both follow. Conti, have your men guard the outside along with the Thing One and Thing Two," I start rushing out orders.

"Pulling up to drop off. Radio silence starts now," Weil speaks into our ears.

The back of the warehouse comes into view, and we stop a good block away. We quietly but quickly make it out of the van and start heading toward the bay door. I notice a door off to the side, and I make the sign to the boys showing them that's the entry point. Waving the others to get into place, we get into our spots.

Two of Conti's men brings in the ram and gets into position. I hold up five fingers and wait for the sign from Weil. We have to make sure we have all points of entry covered and protected before we head inside.

"Go."

I glance at Ghost and nod that we are a go, then start to count down from five, letting a finger drop with each second. When I clench my fist, I ready my gun and watch as the boys ram the door down. Without a second thought, I rush into the building after the boys step to the side.

The first thing I spot is Diego, Tray, and three others off to the side by a van.

"Where the fuck are they?"

"What the fuck are you doing here?" Tray screams.

"Where's my woman and sister?" I watch them but not a one starts to talk. "You got five seconds to answer me or I'm going to start putting bullets in your bodies."

"Careful, Neil. Let's get them alive if we can," Weil speaks into my ear.

I spot one of the other guys reach behind him, and that's all the signal I need. Pulling the trigger, I spot Diego and Tray hitting the ground. They know I'm not playing games. Before the other three even know what happened, they're on the ground, blood pouring out of them.

"Not asking again, so you better answer me or you will be like your friends lying next to you," I say in an eerily calm voice.

"Shit, who is still alive?" Weil questions.

"Diego and Tray so far," Ghost murmurs back.

Tray slowly raises his hand and points to a door toward the back of the room. Glancing to my right, I watch as Conti and a few of his men descend on Diego and Tray. Not waiting another moment, I rush to the door they pointed out.

"Get an ambulance here. They confirmed the women are here," Conti speaks into my ear.

"Affirmative. Ambulance is on the way," Weil confirms back.

Ghost has the door open before I can fully reach it. I spot Len's head on Sara's lap, and there's a guy kneeling next to her. When he looks up at us, I'm thrown for a loop at who I'm staring at. I recognize this guy from the bar the other night.

"What in the ever-loving fuck?" Ghost roars out, spotting him at the same time.

"Dante, please. The babies are coming. We don't have

time. Sara . . . fuck this hurts . . . she passed . . . ughhhhhh . . . out," Len grunts out between panting breaths, which causes Dante to run to her side.

"Get the fuck away from her, Rome." My voice is deadly and he glances back at me.

"Hands in the air and step away from Sara," Conti says from behind me.

Following orders, he puts the gun down gently, stands, and walks away from her. I glance at Conti, and see that him and Nicoli and Carlo have him covered, then rush to Sara's side.

"*Habibti,* wake up, love," I murmur to her while gently shaking her and looking her over.

"Ambulance is here. Another is en route," Conti sounds out as he's walking a cuffed Rome out the door.

The next few moments are a blur as they load Len onto a gurney and start to wheel her out. Looking down, I still don't understand why she isn't waking up. I watch as the second set of EMTs are checking her vitals over.

"Why isn't she waking up yet?" The anguish is thick in my voice as I worry about what is going on.

"We aren't sure yet, sir. Let's load her and get her to the hospital."

"I'm going with her."

"Sir, are you family?"

"I'm her fucking man, so yes I'm fucking family. The only damn family she has." The last word is choked out as I try to hold back my emotions and stay strong.

"Good enough. Let's roll."

Following behind them, I find myself praying. Something that I don't do often. But maybe, just maybe, the big guy will listen and not take her from me yet.

Twenty-Four

Sara

"SARA." I GLANCE BACK OVER at the doctor that's sitting across from me.

I didn't want to be here, not again. After I came to in the hospital, they did everything to get me to talk. Nothing—I had nothing. All I could think of was that Neil was gone, and I wish I was gone with him. Two hours of the doctors prodding and poking, then I heard his voice and I just lost it.

I was now hearing things, is the only thought that came to mind. I closed my eyes and allowed the tears to just come forward. Then when I felt those familiar hands on my body, I knew I'd lost it for good. There's no way they would ever consider me sane when I explain that now I feel his touch.

It took another two hours before I realized he really was alive. But by then the doctors diagnosed me as catatonic and medically admitted me into the mental floor that's part of the hospital. That was two days ago, and I'm so ready to leave this place. I didn't like being in a place like this the last time, and this time is no different.

"Sara, are you ready to talk about the nightmares?" Dr. Bare asks.

"No," I whisper, which causes her to shake her head at me.

"Sara, I know you don't want to be here. You want to get out of here, and I understand. But that isn't going to happen until you start participating in the activities and your therapy sessions with me. So—your choice when you can leave."

I stare right at her with a blank expression. I just want to see Neil. I want to go home.

"Oh, and no visitors either until then. Now, our time is up. Next time we talk, right?"

My heart sinks, knowing that I'm going to have to open up, and I'm just not ready for that. Rolling my eyes, I stand and walk out of the office. I head to the lounge area and take a seat on one of the couches there. I hate that they lock the rooms that hold our beds during the day.

I see a guy named Gus make his way to me holding a piece of paper. A lot of people here don't like him because he has been diagnosed with schizophrenia, but I actually enjoy his company. He has always been such a nice guy and allows me to be me. He's also a very talented artist. I think it just has to do with the mix of people in here.

That's the thing with this place—I'm in for depression, and yet I'm mixed with people who have real medical mental issues. It can be scary at times. Hell, last night a guy decided to try and cut his wrist because the woman who truly believes she is Reba wouldn't marry him. This is just another reason why I want out of here.

"Hey, Red," Gus says as he sits down next to me.

"Hi, Gus. How are you today?"

"Good. The guy says to stop."

"What guy, Gus?" I ask him.

"The angel that has been guarding you for a while now, I guess. He said stop dwelling on the past and what could have happened. It's time to move on. There are bigger things out there waiting for you."

I'm confused at what he's saying so I just sit there and close my eyes. After about an hour I feel him tap on my arm. I must have fallen asleep again while he was doing his drawing.

"Remember, you need to stop." He stands and hands me the drawing and walks off.

Watching him walk away, I smile softly. He's always giving me his drawings and honestly, I love them. My eyes scan the paper, and my breath catches in my throat.

How? What? No, it can't be . . .

There in black and white, with what looks like a light shining behind him, is Arturo staring at me with his signature smirk in place. Tears are forming, and I know it's time to get my act together. I look past his shoulder, and there are my parents looking back and smiling along with Mauricio and Rupert. At that, I can't stop the sobs that come out of my mouth. I want to make them proud, and I just got the push I needed to get out of here and start my life with Neil. I just hope it isn't too late.

NEIL

It has been four days since I had to leave Sara at the hospital. Everything in me screamed not to, but I know the doctors were worried about her mental health. And honestly, so was I.

It took two hours to calm her down after she heard my voice. She kept whimpering, crying, and repeating that I was dead. I tried everything from talking to her, holding her, kissing her forehead, and even attempted leaving, but that made her even worse when she couldn't feel or hear me anymore. The doctors kept repeating the term catatonic, and I kept praying she would snap out of it.

They decided she needed to be admitted to the mental floor, and right before they whisked her away, she looked at me and said, "You really are alive. Oh, God, thank you," then started bawling even harder. I tried to talk the doctors out of admitting her since she recognized that I was finally alive. However, they argued that the PTSD she was suffering from because of the last trauma she witnessed, and now this, was too much and she needed help. Reluctantly, I agreed after Chris came and explained it more to me.

He also suggested I seek some counseling for not only what happened this time, but also for what happened with Len and with what happened on our last mission. As I walked up to check in on Len, Ghost, and the twins, I contemplated what he said and decided he's right.

I spent about two hours with my sister and the twins while Ghost went home to take a shower and check on Little Man. My nephew and niece are so cute, and they make me want a child with Sara soon. Both look just like their brother, Marcus. My poor sister has to deal with none of her kids looking like her. The decided on the names Thomas Anthony and Jaye Ann, still keeping that tradition that Pops started a long time ago with my and Len's name.

After hogging and holding my niece and nephew, I talked to Len about me seeking help for PTSD and what she thought. She explained that Chris was right and she knew of a good therapist here at the hospital she could recommend that would help. She also said it might do some good for Sara and I to go as a couple every once in a while so we can learn each other's triggers.

The day after Sara was admitted, I showed up at the hospital to visit her. However, I was told she wasn't allowed visitors and they were not sure when she would be allowed them. So, after visiting my sister and the babies again, I went and made an appointment with the therapist my sister recommended.

Now, I've been hitting the gym trying to control my desire to go and drag Sara out of there just so I can spend one minute with her. It's driving me crazy because they can't tell me shit since I'm not on any paperwork or family. Rubbing my jeans and feeling the ring has me thinking that's going to change very quickly if I can help it.

The sound of my phone ringing pulls me out of my thoughts of Sara walking down the aisle to me. Seeing it's the hospital has my heart beating out of my chest.

"Shields."

"Mr. Shields, this is Dr. Bare. I'm calling to see if you're free this afternoon for a session with Sara and me."

"Of course, what time? And what is this session for?"

"Sara would like you to join in the last ten minutes of a therapy session with me. We both feel that if you're contemplating being a part of her life, then you need to come and listen to her concerns and to also learn a few things to help with her PTSD triggers. And it will be between four and four thirty."

I take a deep breath because there's no contemplating about it. She's mine.

"I'll be there." Hanging up, I take a glance at the clock. I have two hours until I finally get to see her.

"Welcome, Mr. Shields. Please have a seat," Doctor Bare greets me and points to a chair that's opposite where Sara is.

"Please, call me Neil." I shake her hand, then walk right up to Sara and kneel in front of her. "Habibti, I've missed you, baby."

When her eyes meet mine and I see the tears form, my heart breaks and I can't hold back anymore. I reach out and snatch her out of her chair and hold her close to me.

"Sara, please don't cry. It's going to be okay. We'll work through whatever. I'm not going anywhere," I whisper gently in her ear.

"Neil. I . . . I'm s . . . o sorry," she shudder-sobs out.

"No need to be sorry, Habibti. We got this, love. Now, deep breaths. That's it. Let's get this done so I can spend some time with you, okay?"

I pull back and look in her eyes. When she gives me a small smile, I can't stop myself. I crash my lips to hers and kiss her deeply, pouring out all the love I can muster from my soul into it. The sound of a cough has me slowing and ending it way faster than I wanted to.

"Neil. Sara. I know you both missed each other, but we need to get through this session. Now, let's talk triggers."

And like that . . . the rest of the session was concentrated on Sara and her needs for when she comes out of here.

Twenty-Five

NEIL

One Month Later . . .

IT'S BEEN A MONTH, AND things have been slowly getting better. Today I know is going to be a hard day for Sara. It's trial day. The only blessings I can say from that are two things.

One, Sara and Len don't have to testify at the trial. Their doctors wrote a letter stating that it would be more detrimental to their mental health if they were to go and give their testimony in person, and that their video statements were going to have to do. The lawyer and judge agreed, seeing as they were going up on multiple counts of murder, attempted murder, kidnapping, attempted human trafficking, and multiple drug charges. For the murder charges alone, they're facing multiple life sentences and possibly death sentence.

Two, they're off the streets and no longer a worry for us. However, Sara is still scared about the cartel coming after her, even though Weil and Rome let it be known that wasn't a worry. And knowing Rome was working with Weil undercover as an informant was the shocker of a lifetime. He took a deal when he was caught in a case that would have been bad for him, so they offered him to work with the FBI for immunity on all charges and the chance for a new life when it was over.

That, I think, shocked us the most. I honestly hope he gets that chance because I think he was dealt a bad hand in life.

"Hey, any update on the trial?" Eagle asks as he walks into my office.

"Nope, just waiting for a phone call from Conti. Heard from Sin lately?"

"Not yet. I called him earlier and he didn't answer. I don't know if he's on an op with Mace or Coleman, or if he's just ignoring me. I need to know when he's heading back."

"Did we find out the girl's name?"

"All I got out of him was MaryAnn. He won't tell me a last name just yet," Doc pipes up from the door. "I also called him today and told his ass that if he doesn't call by the end of the day, I was flying in."

This causes us all to chuckle because I swear those two are always competing and fighting over something.

"What are you going to do, drag him back here like a momma bear would her cub? Ground him for spending time with a girl? Are you missing your boy, Doc?" Ghost teases, walking into my office behind him.

"Your hand getting its workout since your butt buddy is still missing in action? You know Andy would jump at the chance to help you with your problem."

"You guys are assholes," Doc mumbles out and stomps

over to my coffee station.

"Your just upset because . . ." My phone ringing has us sobering up.

"Shields."

"It's Conti. Both Diego and Tray got the death penalty. It's done."

Fuck, yes!

That's what I needed to hear. Now it's time to go break the news to my girl and then show her the future we're going to have.

Walking into the house, I hear music blaring out and I smile to myself. She's having a good day today. I've noticed that if music is playing, then she had a great day. If it's quiet, then that means it was a hard day and she's probably in the study reading her books.

I follow the sound of music, and the sight that greets me almost has me dropping to my knees.

Sara is dancing while she's cooking dinner, however I can't even begin to describe how fucking sexy her attire is. She's in one of my old Navy T-shirts and some sexy-ass knee-high black stockings. Her back is to me, and I notice she has her hair in one of those messy-ass buns on the top of her hair which is showing off her sexy neck that I want to lick and bite.

We haven't had sex since the morning of the signing. I was leaving it up to her to give me the sign that she was ready. I'm hoping that after I give her the ring that's in my pocket tonight, she'll give me the go.

The music changes, and she squeals and start singing along. The song that came on is perfect for this vision in front of me. *Thomas Rhett; T-shirt.*

When the chorus comes on, I make my way up to her and grab her hips, pulling her to me.

"Neil!"

"Keep dancing, *Habibti.* You're making me hard as fuck seeing you move this sexy body and wearing just my T-shirts and stockings. Are you giving me a hint, Sara?" I murmur into her ear before licking the edge of it.

"Yes . . . I thought that since . . . mmmm, *Habibi,*" she moans.

"You thought what?"

"Since we got the news about the trial . . . we could . . . oh, God, don't stop," she pants as I run my hands up her thighs slowly, taking my shirt with it.

"Keep talking, *Habibti,* or I'll stop. Conti called you?"

"Yes . . . he told me the news . . . yes right there," she demands when I start to slowly trace a finger up and down her drenched panties. "So, we need to celebrate and I have news of my own . . . fuck!"

Chuckling at the fact she's losing her train of thought as I gently push her panties aside and start to play with her clit, I decide now is the time.

"Marry me."

Her gasp, and the fact that her hands grab my arms stopping me, lets me know that she heard me.

"What did you just say?"

"Marry me," I demand again, pulling my hand back, then digging into my pocket to pull out the ring.

I continue to kiss her neck as I reach around her,

opening my hand that's holding it. Her gasp lets me know she sees what is in my palm.

"Neil . . ." It's barely a whisper.

"I don't want to wait anymore. I need you in my life permanently. We both know life is short. So, say yes."

"Yes."

Quickly I turn her to face me and place the ring on her left hand.

"It's beautiful. When did you get it?"

"I picked it out shortly after you left the first time. I had it engraved, but you can look at it later. I need you now."

"Neil . . . wait. I need to tell you something," she says while she stops me from pulling my T-shirt off her.

Looking up into her eyes, I see the tears forming and I can't help but wonder if she already changed her mind.

Sara

The look of panic on Neil's face make my breath catch in my throat.

"Sara, please tell me you didn't already change your mind? If you did, I won't accept it. You're officially stuck to me for life. I will even get paperwork drawn up and make it look like you signed your damn name."

His determination on his face and his words have me erupting in giggle.

"*Habibti*, if you don't tell me right now what is bothering you or what news you have to tell me, then I'm going to throw you over my shoulder, and then take you to our bed to fuck it out of you."

That did it. I'm now full-on laughing at him. I can't help it–he took the nerves away with his caveman act . . . okay, it isn't an act, but it cracks me up that he thinks he can just sign my name on paperwork, and I'm his for life.

I'm flying and on his shoulder before I can even catch my next breath. He quickly shuts off the stove and oven before turning and heading toward the stairs. I smack him on his ass and laughing at his playfulness.

Smack!

"Ouch, Neil!"

He chuckles as he makes it to our bedroom while he's rubbing the sting from my ass that he just smacked. Then he tosses me on our bed.

"Now, you want to share this 'news' you have for me?"

I squeeze my eyes shut and then take a deep breath.

"We have to get married quickly because I don't want to be fat in my wedding dress since-I'm-pregnant-with-your-baby," I quickly mumble out, then cringe because I wasn't wanting to drop it out like that.

Silence is all I'm met with. Shit, I feared this happening. I know he's going to flip out on me since this isn't planned. Taking another deep breath, I take a chance and peek out between my lashes at him. His face is emotionless, and he's staring right at my face.

"Neil," is barely a whisper out of my mouth.

"What did you say?"

"Um, which part didn't you understand?"

"It sounded like you were demanding we get married fast because you believe you're going to be fat because you're pregnant with my baby. Is that what you said?"

Tears are starting to form because I don't know what to think of how he worded it.

"Yeah, I mean . . . every girl dreams of getting married. And I'm not ashamed of being pregnant before marriage. I just don't want to have a huge fat ass or look like a beached white whale on my wedding day and then have pictures that show it. I want my pictures to be beautiful, so if we are going to do this then we have to do it fast because I found out today I'm eight weeks pregnant. I got pregnant because they gave me antibiotics when I was in the hospital and it countered . . . What are you doing?" I squeal out as he pushes up my shirt and then nudges his way between my legs so he can lay down.

"Daddy is so fucking . . . shit . . . da . . . dang it. Daddy needs to learn to watch his cussing. Now, as I was saying . . . Daddy is so freaking happy that your sexy mommy has you in her belly. You will learn she has verbal vomit when she gets riled up, but that's okay because she's a pretty amazing person. And knowing she's protecting you in her belly while you grow, I love you so much already," he whispers the ending, then kisses my stomach right by my belly button. "Now, go to sleep so I can have Mommy time, *ya binti*."

I bust up laughing, but my heart is filled with love with how he talked to our little one.

"What does that mean?" I ask as he slowly starts making his way up my body with kisses.

"It means daughter," he murmurs and then latches onto one of my nipples that he just exposed.

"The baby could be a boy . . . easy . . . they're sensitive."

"Then I will call him, *ya ibni*. But you're having my daughter first. I've always wanted a little daddy's girl."

"Most men want their boy first, then a girl . . . mmm, don't stop," I moan when he takes my other nipple.

"I'm not most men–haven't you realized that yet, Habibti? Now, no more baby talk . . . it's Mommy and Daddy time."

"Mommy and Daddy time," I quickly agree, and he proceeds to show me just how much me being pregnant and accepting his proposal means to him for the rest of the night.

Twenty-Six

NEIL

I JUST SHAKE MY HEAD at watching Sara out on the dance floor shaking her ass with her girls to Theory of a Deadman's "Bad Girlfriend." She turns her head slightly, stares at me while she sings the chorus, then winks at me and turns back toward her circle.

We got married today, and I can't help but be grateful that we were able to do it quickly. It's two weeks after we got engaged, and we had a small family affair. She didn't have many people to invite, so she didn't want her side to be so small. We decided to have it in my parents' backyard, and it was beautiful. However, the family wasn't happy that they had to rush the details. We decided we would wait until right before we left for our honeymoon to announce that we were pregnant.

"Please clear the floor for a special requested dance that Mr. Shields is wanting with Mrs. Shields," the DJ announces.

The familiar chords, to that one song starts to play, and I

see Sara start giggling as she turns to me.

"Really, *Habibi*?"

"What can I say? The song left an amazing memory in my head and now whenever I hear it, I get an instant hard on for my wife."

"T-shirt?"

"Like I said . . . it holds some fucking amazing memories of my wife dancing in nothing but my T-shirt," I murmur into her ear and rub my hard cock against her, causing her to moan.

"Can we leave after this?"

"You ready to go home so I can make you my wife officially?"

"Yes," she whimpers.

She's fucking horny, so much more since finding out she's pregnant. And trust me when I say I don't fucking mind one bit. I now can make her come from messing with her breasts alone. Thinking of making her scream my name later has me ready to pick her up bridal style and running out the door. There's clapping all around us, making me realize that the song is over, which makes me smile because that means it's time.

"Ready?"

With a nod, I grab her hand and drag her to the DJ booth. She's laughing, but she has no clue what little control I now have. I'm ready to make love to my wife for the first time. I think ten hours without being in her is enough. My mom tried to get us to sleep apart, but yeah, I wasn't having that bullshit. I adore and respect my mom, but I told her that when Sara came home from the hospital this time that there wasn't ever going to be another night apart. Then my mom cried and said she's so happy that both her kids found love like her and Pops. And that's when I tuned out and just let her have her crying fest.

I wave at the DJ for the microphone and then turn to our guests, Sara's hand still in my grasp.

"Thanks for coming while I make this beautiful woman mine for life. I feel I definitely got the better end of this marriage deal we just made." I smile down at her and see her nod her head at me while she's laughing.

"See, she agrees. Now, we have an announcement to make, then I'm taking my *Habibti* back home so I can finally . . ." is all I can get out before she jerks the microphone out of my hand. "What?"

"Don't even think about it," she sternly tells me, then turns back to the crowd who is laughing at my antics. "Anyway, as my perverted husband was saying before he decided to say things he shouldn't . . ."

"It isn't like they don't know what will happen tonight, *Habibti*. Everyone knows what people do on their wedding night."

The crowds start making catcalls and whistling at my words, which has me chuckling until I feel an elbow in my side.

"Just for that, I'm going to stay with Momma Connie and Pops tonight while you go home alone," she states loudly into the microphone.

"You're always welcome, new daughter of mine," Pops states with humor lacing his voice. He knows that shit isn't happening.

"Go ahead and just watch what happens when my parents are awakened because their new daughter is . . ." is all I can get out before I feel a slap to the back of my head and see my mom walked up to my other side.

"Son, stop while you're ahead. Now, what is your announcement, Sara?" Mom asks.

"Well, Neil and I want to announce that in about thirty weeks, we'll be adding to our family."

The screams, squeals, cheers, whoops, and hollers drown out Sara's laughter at their reaction. And that somewhat pisses me off because her laughter is a sound I love to hear.

"Let's go hurry while they're celebrating. If we don't leave now, then it will be another hour because everyone is going to want to congratulate us," I whisper into her ear.

"Too late, big brother! I'm going to be an Auntie!" Len squeals and grabs Sara from my arms.

"Congrats, brother! Welcome to the Daddy club. And good luck getting out of here at a decent time now," Ghost chuckles out as he gives me a manly hug.

Great. Just fucking great.

Sara

It's about another hour and a half before we finally made it out of the reception. I know Neil was eager to get home, but we had to allow our friends and family to give us their congrats and share in the happiness. Now, we are home and we have an early flight in the morning to go on our honeymoon–two weeks in Italy at the De Luca's winery. It was their wedding gift to us, and I'm thrilled because I've always wanted to go visit Italy.

When we reach the front door, he scoops me up and carries me over the threshold. Gently sitting me down, he turns and locks the house up as I slowly make my way toward the stairs. Just as I reach the top, I feel his hand on my hips and his lips against my hairline.

"*Habibti*, I know you're exhausted, but I've got to have you," Neil murmurs against my neck as we make our way to our room.

"Can I tell you something first?"

"If it isn't how much you want my cock in your tight pussy, then it can wait."

"Neil, I'm serious. I have a surprise for you."

"Whatever you're wearing under this fucking sexy ass dress is enough of a surprise for me."

He starts to unzip me, and I can feel his tongue trace where the zipper was, and any thought of what I needed to tell him went out of my brain. Before I realize it, my dress is pooled at my feet and Neil is kneeling behind me kissing my ass where my white lacy cheek boy shorts end and my skin begins.

"*Habibti,* I fucking love your ass."

"Neil," is all I can moan out.

"Feet up, wife. Let's get you out of these heels."

He makes quick work of taking off my shoes, then picks me up and carries me to the bed. His hands go to my hips again, and I hear the sound of lace ripping as he tears my panties off my body.

God, that's so fucking hot.

"I'm glad you think so," he chuckles out before he climbs up onto the bed between my legs.

"I said that out loud?"

"Uh-huh. Now, I need to eat dessert. That small bite of cake you gave me wasn't enough, wife of mine," he murmurs against my thigh.

"Well, husband of mine, don't let me stop you from getting your fill of dessert," I moan out as he nips his way to my pussy.

"Oh, don't worry, Habibti, nothing is stopping me."

He descends quickly and slowly starts to lick me. God, it feels so fucking good, and I know I'm going to come quickly. I'm too worked up.

He licks and nips over and over until I'm clutching his hair tightly in my fist.

"Come on, Sara. Come for me."

He sucks my clit into his mouth and I need just a bit more–I'm so on edge. Then I feel his fingers enter me, and I shatter.

When I finally come down from my high, Neil is above me and smiling down at me with my juices still covering his lower face.

"You're so beautiful when you come," he softly says as he lines himself up with my opening and slowly enters me. "Fuck, you're always so fucking tight."

I reach up and bring his mouth to me and lick his lips. Tasting myself on him when he enters me makes me even wetter.

"Fuck your wife, Neil. I need it hard and fast. Don't hold back," I say against his lips.

He growls out before he sits up, grabs my hips, and starts to thrust hard and fast into me.

"Yes! Harder, husband. Harder!" I moan out loudly.

"Fuck . . . hearing the words wife and husband come

from your lips . . . fuck. Remember I love you, Sara. Because after I'm done fucking you tonight . . . you're going to wonder if I do."

His hips move faster than they ever have, and his thrusts are hard and punishing. He wasn't lying–if I didn't know he loved me more than anything in this world, I would swear he hated me with the way he's fucking me right now.

"Oh, God. I'm going to come."

"Fuck . . . come, baby. Come on my cock. I need to feel you clench me as I empty inside my wife for the first time," he groans out.

The combination of his thrusts, voice, and hearing the word *wife* out of his mouth sets me off, and I come hard.

"Yes, Sara, milk me, baby. Fuck . . ." he screams out and thrusts four more times before he stills, and I feel his cum explode out of his cock.

He falls over to the side, taking me with him, and holds me to his side as we come down from our shared orgasm.

"Mrs. Shields, it's official now."

"Hmmm . . . that reminds me of what I was going to tell you."

"What's that?"

I take a deep breath. "I filed for a name change with our marriage license."

"Okay, we knew that was part of it," he murmurs sleepy.

"No, I also picked the name I want to be called from now on."

He sits up and looks down at me.

"Okay, which name did you decide on?"

"Sara Marie Shields. But if we have a little girl, can we use Rebecca as either her first or middle name? I don't feel like Rebecca anymore, but I don't want to forget that name. My parents loved me, and I feel that by giving it to our daughter, then it's carrying on their memory."

"I love that idea, baby, and I'm glad you figured out which name you want to go with. Now, let's get some rest. We have two weeks ahead of us to work out all the details of names." He leans down and gives me a soft kiss.

"Ahebbouka aktar men ayga, Habibti."

"Ahebbouka aktar men ayga, Habibi."

Epilogue

JAKE DUVAL

Eight Months Later . . .

***

"WHAT ARE WE DOING HERE, Uncle Jake?" Kristian asks as we are both looking around the hospital corridor we currently find ourselves walking down.

"I don't know, kiddo. Do you see your mother or your Aunt Faith anywhere?"

"No, but there is a bunch of people talking in that room." He points toward the upcoming room.

"Oh, Julia, look! She's beautiful!" The sound of Julia's name catches my attention.

"Sounds like your mother is in there." I motion to the room Kristian had just pointed to. "Let's go see who the new member of our family is."

Together, we make our way into the room. Inside, the room is filled to capacity with men and women surrounding a hospital bed and passing around a small wrapped bundle. Scanning the faces, I look for Julia but don't see her, nor do I see Faith or any person I recognize.

"Julia! Hand her over," sounds from one of the men in the room. My eyes go to the woman in question with the much-coveted baby. "Stop hogging her."

"Fine," she sighs dramatically. "I'll share." She hands the baby over, and they all continue to ooh and ahh.

"Who are all these people, Uncle Jake?" Kristian whispers the question, though it's unnecessary since no one can see us.

"I don't know, Kristian. L . . . let's get out of here." But trying to leave the room is impossible—I'm rooted to the floor. This is the second time this has happened to me. With that thought in mind, I take a closer look at all the faces, and my body goes still with shock. Lying in the hospital bed is that girl, and now a woman.

"Uncle Jake! What are you doing? What's happening?" Kristian asks, alarmed, as he too seems to be unable to leave the room.

"Shhh . . ." Holding up a finger to silence him, I continue toward her. There has to be a reason why we're here. There has to be a reason why I couldn't leave her then, and I can't leave her now.

Standing at her bedside, the baby is handed back to her. Craning my neck to get a better look, I find clear, cerulean blue eyes staring back at me. As if seeing me, the baby graces me with a smile. That smile hits me like a ton of bricks, and a sharp pang strikes my heart as I realize—this is the reason I saved her. I'm here for the baby . . .

More To Me
More Series Book 3
Doc and Ashley's
Story coming Spring/Summer 2017 Continue
reading for a special bonus chapter

Bonus Chapter

JAKE DUVAL

Ten Years Ago . . .
***

ONE MOMENT, I'M TRYING TO adjust to my new living conditions and figuring out what the hell I'm supposed to do to help my loved ones, because that's what I was informed was my new mission as a guardian, and the next I feel as if I'm flying through space at the speed of light before being roughly jerked to a stop. The stop is so sudden that my head whips forward and then back, making me wonder if whiplash is a possible outcome.

Shit! With one hand, I touch my left temple and with the other, I hold the back of my neck and send my gaze upwards. The big Man could have at least given me a warning if I was being sent back down. It was embarrassing that I couldn't even land on my feet.

Quickly and carefully, though I feel much better now and my neck feels mobile, I look around my strange surroundings, finding myself in a bedroom.

"Get the fuck in here now!" sounds from the other room, and I hear movement as a man scrambles off the bed. Out of instinct, I try to lower myself out of view. Before I can inspect the room more or get a closer look at the man, who this room must belong to, the blanket flies off the bed with more force than it should have, covering me.

Before I can struggle to get out from underneath, I feel a body beneath me. Looking down, I find myself hovering over a woman trying to squeeze underneath the bed. Quickly, I try to scramble up and away, but my attempts are futile. It's as if I—I'm *stuck* to her. Something, some force, won't let me move or leave, no matter how hard I try. With me over her, she doesn't fit under the bed, which is strange because my presence shouldn't affect anything. I'm nothing . . . in reality, I'm dead, something that has taken much time to get adjusted to and accept, and I sure as hell shouldn't be here. So why the fuck am I still here and keeping her from hiding?

As I'm trying to figure out my situation, the man moves out.

Soon after he walks out and into the next room, there's a loud bang that resonates in my mind. That sound, a sound I know so well having lived with it for over a decade, *that* was a goddamn gunshot.

What the fuck is going on?

Why am I here and with *her*? She's a complete stranger.

As my mind races, more gunshots sound, and I feel her squirm and see her mouth start to open. If they hear her, they'll kill her. These types of people don't leave witnesses, regardless of how young they are and their gender. Especially with her gender, I don't even want to imagine what she'll go through, what he'll do to her, if he finds her. Whatever is going on, whatever she's involved in, I can't let a woman get hurt.

Survival instinct kicks in, and I quickly cover her mouth with my right hand, surprisingly keeping her silent, and hunker down on her. With reassuring words whispered into her ear, ones I know she can't hear, I hope to calm her down. She needs to remain quiet, calm, and alert because that's the only way she'll get out of this alive.

"Is everyone in here?" a deep, male voice sounds, making me think of a crazed and out-of-control person under the influence. His question is followed by a brief pause, probably scanning the room, before continuing, "Good. Now, where are the drugs and money?"

Fucking drugs! That's what this is all about? Looking down at the girl, I shake my head in disappointment that one so young is involved in that sort of nastiness. The drug business is a dangerous, ruthless, and bloody business.

"I don't kno—" Three loud shots cut off the protest and are followed by screams, informing me that there are more people out there besides the man from this room and the madman. Looking at the girl's face, I see she's shut her eyes, as if trying to shut everything that's happening out.

"Again, where are they?" the crazed man asks again.

"Look, this is my apartment." That must the man from this room, "And I have no clue what you're talking about."

"Have it your way," the intruder says eerily, nonchalant before more shots follow, but instead of screams, there are only multiple moans of pain.

"Last time—where are the drugs and money?" the voice demands. Hearing that evil voice and feeling the girl's body shaking, I know for a fact she will remember this moment and that voice for the rest of her life. Traumatizing situations like these tend to stick to you for a lifetime, and are more often than not—life-changing. My hope is, if she survives this, that she changes her way because she has no business in this type of life.

This time, nobody answers the question. As the silence progresses, her body starts to shake harder and wetness covers my hand. She's terrified, and there's nothing I can do. I feel useless and helpless, not knowing exactly what's going on in the next room. All I can assume is that there are bodies filled with bullets scattered throughout the room.

Three more shots followed by screams sound, putting me on alert once again, and informing me the motherfucker is still here. Whatever he's searching for, he isn't finding it. Whatever the reason for me being here, whether I like it or not, I need to look after this girl.

As more shots sound, the agonizing screams that follow start withering down to moans, one by one, and then they go heavily quiet. I can only pray that whatever power is keeping me here with her helps us. That the man hurries the hell up and finds whatever he's searching for, or that he gives up and leaves. I can feel my strength waning and pretty soon, I won't be able to hold her down . . .

Ten Years Later - Explosion . . .

Goddamn it! I hate when shit like this happens. Normally, the big Man gives me a heads up when he's sending me somewhere, but not this time. Closing my eyes, I brace myself for the sudden, jerky stop that I know is coming.

However, this time is different. One moment, I'm flying through space at high speed, and the next, and I find myself flying in slow motion through the air before coming to a gentle stop in front of two handcuffed women. My first thought is, "Damn it, not again." Having just dealt with a madwoman kidnapping and almost killing my wife's best friend, I don't fancy seeing that happen again.

Kneeling down to their level, I get a closer look but neither is Faith or Julia or Rylee, causing me to sigh in relief. Though, the questions arise. Who are they, and why am I here? Both are strangers, though one of the women looks vaguely familiar. Before I can inspect either one further or take in anything else besides the two of them, a voice sounds from the other room.

"What the fuck did you think we were going to do, Walters? Have a goddamn tea party and bake cookies with her?" That voice is one I won't forget. That voice belongs to the motherfucker I encountered years ago, and suddenly it all makes sense. Looking back at the women, my gaze moves to one woman in particular. Inspecting her further, I see it's *her*, the one from years ago, the stranger I saved. "She saw something she shouldn't have seen and can put me and my men away for life," the lunatic practically yells at Walters, and everything falls into place. So, she did change her ways, that's why she looks so different from the last time I saw her.

The other woman tugs at her arms, and her eyes crack open. "Bomb," the other woman mouths, causing my stomach to fall.

The door suddenly opens, and I see her eyes widen in fear. Quickly, I settle beside her and stroke her hair reassuringly as I whisper calming words into her ear. Her eyes close, and I feel her body relax. All the while, my mind is racing, trying to find a way to save both women. If there's a bomb involved, I'm in over my head.

"Timer is set. Let's get the fuck out of here and far enough away to watch the explosion."

Damn it! They're leaving. That means shit's about to go up in flames. Hearing the door shutting, informing me the damn cowards have run, my heart pounds in my ears, and I have to take a few calming breathes myself.

"Come on, Sara. We have to get out of here," The other woman's words jerk me out of my stunned state.

Giving them a gentle surge of energy, the women move, and I have to chuckle at the stupidity of the men. They didn't handcuff them to the bed—this will make escaping so much easier. As the other woman fishes in her pockets and comes up empty handed, I have to admit the men aren't as dumb as I thought they were—they took the key. Though it will hinder the escape slightly, it's not a lost cause.

As much as I can help them, I aid them in struggling out of the bed and stumbling into the other room. As the other woman outlines her plan of escape, I stay close to my charge, especially after the baffled look on her face at the words, "Run east," and her brief question.

Crossing the doorway out of the house, I see a man running in our direction. Expecting a gunshot, I try to shield the women as best as I can before my charge calls out, "Conti, stop there's a—"

Suddenly, a force of pressure sends us soaring through the air, as a loud, eardrum-shattering explosion sounds. Searing heat, smoke, and pressure waves follow as I try to lessen our impact as much as possible. As my attention is divided between both women, I fail in my primary mission: making sure my charge is unharmed. Before I can fully wrap myself around her, we hit the ground, and her head slams on the asphalt. Though I helped lessen the impact, her head still bounces slightly with the impact, causing a sense of failure to engulf me.

Through the ongoing chaos around us and the aftermath of the explosion, I cradle her face and pray that she's okay. Hovering over her, I see her eyes open and focus on me before her eyes close and her head falls to the side as the whispered words, "Neil . . . love . . . please . . ." fall from her lips.

Please, God, save her, I plead up to the big Man. I can't have another death on my hands. I tried my best to save both of them. Please, save her.

As I plead for her life and she's ripped from my arms, all I can think is, *she saw me*, and my heart falls.

The Epi and Bonus Chapters were written by ML Rodriguez. Jake is from her series La Flor. We'll be collaborating on a book in the future, and this is part of that story. Make sure you check out her books so when we collaborate, you're caught up and know what is going on.

Added Bonus Scene

Dear Sara:

Tomorrow is your wedding day, and I know you have a surprise planned to tell Neil the name you

have chosen to go by. I want you to know that you will always be Rebecca . . . just an older version. You will keep the name alive when you share the story of your parents and your childhood with the child growing inside you and with your future children.

Your parents would be and are proud of the person you have become. Never doubt that or forget that you were loved fiercely by them . . . no matter if you do choose to be called Sara.

You're a strong person and a true survivor. Now, it's time to retire this journal and live the life you were meant to live.

-Rebecca <3

Continue Reading for the preview of book three . . . More To Me – More Series Book Three

Acknowledgements

Wow there are so many people I need to think for this amazing journey. I know I'll end up forgetting someone so in advance if I forget you, I'm sorry. I didn't do it intentionally!

First and always will be **God**. Without him in my life, I'm nothing.

My Hubs: I honestly lucked out in the husband department when I married you almost seventeen years ago. Thank you for the constant support and for being my biggest cheerleader. Even if you're halfway around the world. I'm looking forward to you getting out of the military and spending every night in your arms. I love you. One More Time xoxo <3

My Kids: Thank you for being the most amazing teens a Mom could ask for. I tell everyone often just how lucky I am to have two of the most amazing children ever. Thanks for letting Mom write. Also for repeating yourselves often when I'm writing and you're trying to talk to me. <3

My Family: Thank you for supporting me and giving me so much love on taking this journey. After my first book having you all reach out with congrats and wanting to read my book, I wasn't expecting it. Thanks for making me smile and for the love you give me. I hope you all enjoy this book just as much as you did book one. <3

Mari: You're such an amazing friend and I'm grateful that God brought you into my life. Thank you for the support and constant help when I'm stuck with something in my writing. I can honestly say I'm excited for the collab we are going to do in the future. I love you to pieces and look forward to margarita nights. <3 #BubbleSisters

Lynne aka My Sister/Friend/HLM4L: Jesus what can I say that I haven't already told you? You're the crazy to my calm and yet my calm to my crazy. I can't imagine with my life would be without you and little man in it. I'm so happy that I adopted myself into your family, because yeah lets be real . . . that's the way it really happened. I love you and little man tons and bunches. Thanks for always being you and loving me for me. <3 #Sisters #TheAmyToMyTina #Legit

Beef: You're one of the few people that I can't go a day without some sort of contact. I get withdrawals if we haven't

chatted after a few hours. That's kind of a scary thought. Thank you for being such an amazing person and for always being a voice of reason when Nutty and I are being crazy. And for being there when I need another Mom to talk to when it comes to Autism meltdowns or just needing to vent about not understanding things with it. I love you and look forward to growing our friendship even more. P.S. Chiefs Cheerleader not Dallas <3 #CMMFS #BestBitches #2018GirlsWeekend #Mrs.S.FuckingCline

Kacey & Keshia: First, thank you for allowing me to mention your names in my book. It means a lot to me. Second, again, thank you for all the advice, checking in with me and helping me with this book too. I can't believe that I'm lucky enough to know you, even if it isn't in person . . . yet. Your guidance and friendship mean more to me then you will ever know. And one day I will be able to show you just how much you both mean to me. <3

Jane aka My Soul Mated Lover: Here we are, another book down! You were my first fan that wasn't an author and who believed in me and my writing. Thank you for everything and for being my soul mated lover. I can't wait to meet you in person one day. Tell K hi for me and we'll talk soon. Love you tons <3

My Crazy Beta's: *Lucy, January, MaryAnn, Laura, Joanne, and Diane:* There's NO way this book could have ever been as good as it without your help. I'm so blessed to

have such an amazing set of beta's. Thank you for all the reads, advice, changes, and putting up with my craziness. I love you guys. Are you ready for book three? <3

Megan: I'm so freaking excited and honored to call you my friend. I'm so grateful that God brought you into my life. You make me smile daily and I now can't imagine what it would be like without you in it. You're an AMAZING author and I honestly am so excited that I will get to watch you explode in the community. You're going to go so far and I'm just excited your allowing me to watch you make your mark on this world. <3

Asshole Panda & Melissa: Yo! Thanks for taking such amazing pictures for me to drool over and then demand I buy, then you make me broke . . . which is an asshole thing to do. But for real, thanks for the friendship and for making me laugh. Who would have thought a friendship could have been made out of a purchase of a picture? Looking forward to what the future holds. #WannaBeFamous #AhPanda #ImTheWorldsBestPsychologist *Melissa:* You set the bar high for me to deliver a book that would capture your attention again. I hope you enjoy this book just as much as you did the first one. I value our friendship and I'm grateful that I'm able to call you my friend. Sorry you have to put up with the asshole a lot. I try my best to keep him in line and yell at him often for you. #YourYoda

Connor aka Sexy Beast: You fit Neil to a T. Thank

you. Also, I'm still waiting on my video of your tic tac challenge. 7 cases?

#wordsprintsisters: I can honestly say there would be no way this book would even be finished if it wasn't for you girls. Thanks for allowing me to join your group and for sprinting at all hours of the day with me. Now, book three! <3

Personal Friends: Thank you for the support you gave me through this. Even if you never read it, know that I appreciate the help you gave me along the way. Special thank you to *Michelle* for being my last read through. I can't thank you enough for the support you give me and having you wanting book two even though this genre isn't your type . . . yeah that meant the world to me. <3 *Rebecca:* Thanks for letting me use your name and your last name . . . surprise?!

Princesa: I love you! You're one of my dearest friends and I'm so damn grateful we got to build our friendship. Thanks for the advice, even if it's harsh at times. I can't thank you enough for everything you have done for me. Now, the trash bags are in the box with this signed paperback I'm sending you. #PrincesasMistress

Jess: Thank you for the endless support and the friendship you give me. I can say I'm blessed to have you in my life and I'm so grateful to call you a friend. I'm looking forward to Feb. I can't wait to road trip with you and also get

that tattoo. This is going to be such a fun weekend! <3 #MistressSonya #KneelForMe #EpicAss #MissouriGirls

Cassia: I can honestly say . . . I don't think we'll have silent convos in person anymore. You're so damn talented that I look up to you in admiration and hope that maybe one day I'll be as talented as you're. I can't wait until Phoenix to give you a hug finally . . . let's just hope we get there in one piece. Don't worry, I'll protect you from falling into the canyon. Thank you for being such an amazing editor/proof reader. Project three is coming soon. <3 #Killer #Lucky #SilentConvoSisters

Eve: You demanded Neil from the start of book one LOL. So here you go babe. He's all yours. Thank you for being such an amazing friend and I'm honored and grateful for all the advice you give me often. <3

Readers: Thank you so much for the overwhelming response you gave me on my first book. I'm really hoping you love this one just as much as you did the first. Thank you for taking that chance again. <3

About The Author

S. Van Horne was born and raised in the small town of Belton, Missouri, which is a part of the Kansas City metropolitan area. She's from a very large family and is the oldest of six. Growing up, she didn't have the easiest life. She learned quickly that family means everything, even if it's the type that you get to pick for yourself.

She met the love of her life at the early age of twenty and was married just after nine months of meeting him. Shortly after marriage, her husband rejoined the U.S. Navy and they moved from Kansas City and started their journey together. Currently they have two amazing children, a boy and a girl, and are still enjoying the Navy life.

She spends her days being a wife, mom, reading books, writing her latest novel, watching her beloved Kansas City Chiefs or Kansas City Royals, watching movies, hanging out with family and friends and having girls' day at least once a month.

CONTACT:

FACEBOOK: S. Van Horne
**FACEBOOK LIKE PAGE: Author S Van
Horne**
**FACEBOOK GROUP: Devils Who Wear
Halos**
GOODREADS: Author S Van Horne
TWITTER: @smvh79
INSTAGRAM: @authorsvan
EMAIL: svanhorne@authorsvanhorne.com
WEBSITE: www.authorsvanhorne.com

Other Books by S.

More Series:
One More Time – Book One
More Than Anything – Book Two
More To Me –Book Three – (Current WIP)
More Than Enough – Book Four (Coming Winter 2017)
Worth Much More – Book Five (Coming Summer 2018)
More Than Air – Book Six (Coming Winter 2018)
More Than Forever – Book Seven (Coming Summer 2019)

More Series Novellas:
More Than Falling – Part of the Passion, Vows and Babies Kindle World
More Than Life (Coming 2018)
More Than Us (Coming 2019)

The Vow Series:
The Vow: Leaving Home– Prequel
The Vow: Jess – Book One – (Current WIP)
The Vow: Shania – Book Two (Spring 2018)
The Vow: Talina – Book Three (Winter 2018)
The Vow: Megan – Book Four (Spring 2019)
The Vow: Cassia – Book Five (Winter 2019)
The Vow: Returning Home (Spring 2020)

Anthologies:
Meat Market Anthology – KC Strip

Tic Tac Challenge

Hello everyone! Andy here and I needed to let you know that the website **http://www.hmttcys.com** is a real site that I created. This website is mentioned in book two. This is where you can now go and tell me just how many Tic Tacs you can swallow if you're up for the challenge. If you're not sure what the challenge is, then make sure you check out S. Van Horne's first book, One More Time. This challenge will now be in each book.

She will also have custom made Tic Tacs that will have this on it as well. There will be a section on the site soon that will also allow you to ask me questions and interact with me. I hope to see your answer soon!

-Andy

More To Me

More To Me – More Series Book Three – Doc and Ashley - Subject to change

Ashley

LOOKING DOWN AT THE BUNDLE in my arms, I can't help but think about my family. About the bomb my parents dropped on me five Christmases ago—the fact that I was adopted and that my adoption was sealed to never be opened, even when I turned of age. I've tried everything I know of to be able to view the information, and I keep hitting dead ends.

I've had a fantastic upbringing, and I adore my adoptive parents. I wouldn't trade my life for anything. However, I've always felt like something was missing, and then there's the fact that I don't look anything like my adoptive parents. I just chalked it up to looking like my great grandparents. DNA coding has proven that a child can get just enough of the genes to make them look just like someone from generations past.

"Ashley, it's my turn. Hand her over!" Julia whines beside me.

"Fine," I murmur and hand her Neil and Sara's little girl. "Are you going to tell us the name now that everyone is here?"

They have been keeping the name quiet, and I'm really wanting to know what they picked. Sara looks at Neil, and he smiles at her, then looks around the room.

"Well, we're keeping up with the tradition that Pops started. So, with that said, her name is Kelce Rebecca Shields."

"That doesn't really flow off the tongue," Doc says, sticking his foot in his mouth yet again.

"James Reginald Hart!" OPG scolds, causing me to giggle. I don't know why, but every time she pulls out the three names on someone, it makes me giggle and I feel like I'm a little girl again. Doc's eyes meet mine, and he gives me a small smirk. I think he does this shit on purpose when I'm around.

We have shared some amazing moments together, and I want to be with him. He hasn't hidden the fact that he wants me, but I really need to find out who I am first before I start a life with someone.

"OPG, it's okay. There's a reason we want Rebecca as the middle name," Sara says, and then explains about wanting to continue the legacy her parents gave her. This causes my mind to go right back to what I was thinking when I was holding little Kelce.

"Well, I think it's a beautiful name. And I have to say nice pick on the player, son. Especially after that amazing reception he had during the Chargers game last Sunday."

I try to smile and pay attention, but my mind just isn't with it. I have this deep need to find my real parents. I just wish I knew where to start after the shitty beginning I've had so far.

DOC

I hear the laughter and conversations going around me, but all I can do is watch Ashley. She has been so depressed lately, and that has me worried about her mental health.

I shouldn't compare her with Lids, but I can't help but think about it. Even though the feeling I have for Ashley surpass what I felt with Lids, I can't help but worry that if I don't keep an eye on things, then I won't be able to stop something from happening.

Then there's the PTSD I still suffer from due to the last mission . . . I'm a fucked-up mess to say the least. But it doesn't stop the desire that I have to make her mine and end this game of cat and mouse we have going on.

"Oh, Julia, look! She's beautiful!" Andy claps his hands together with a look of wonder on his face.

"She really is," Julia murmurs out.

"Julia! Hand her over. Stop hogging her," Andy demands, finally not able to help himself

"Fine," she sighs dramatically. "I'll share."

She hands the baby over, and this causes him to slightly squeal in delight. I swear that guy is a trip. He's always doing shit to make the girls laugh and gives his husband so much shit. But under all that joking, I notice another soul that's like mine. Hurt and pain is deep in him, and he uses humor to deal with the pain. Just like me.

I glance back at Ashley and see she's trying to work something out in her head. I wish she would talk to me about whatever is going through her mind. I've tried to push, but she clams up. The only thing she has ever shared with me is the fact that she's adopted and found out on Christmas Eve five years ago. It gutted her to hear it, and I know she has been trying to find her real family ever since.

"I'm going to head out and get me something to drink. Anyone want anything?" she asks as she stands. I'd recognize that look anywhere because I do it when things get overwhelming and I need a moment to myself.

"Yes, I would like some snacks and drinks. Sara, here's this little angel back, I need to get some money for Ashley," Andy states.

As Sara gets settled with Kelce in her arms, there's a brief chill in the room and the little angel opens her eyes. The color is a beautiful blue, and she smiles just a bit. She's staring right past her mom, right at the wall. *That's odd.*

Everyone starts to call out their orders as Ashley types them on her phone. Once she gets the list, she turns to walk out the door.

"I'll come along and help you carry it back up."

"No, I'm good." She walks out the door without waiting for me.

"I swear to God," I murmur and head toward the door.

"She's going to give you a run for your money, James. You have your hands full trying to show her just what she means to you. She needs to know that someone is going to pick her over anything and anyone," Mamma Gio states as she moves so I can get to the door.

"Mamma Gio, what she doesn't realize and what I'm going to prove is that she means more to me. Showing her that she means that will be easy, it's just getting her to open her eyes to what is in front of her."

She nods and smiles at me, knowing I mean what I say. I turn and head out the door and hear in a soft whisper that I swear is Lids voice, "She's worth it. Now, get to work, James."

Preview Imperfectly Beautiful

Imperfectly Beautiful

(Book Two, La Flor Series)

By: ML Rodriguez

Copyright 2015-2016 to ML Rodriguez

Available Now

"NOTHING'S IMPOSSIBLE AND THINGS AREN'T gonna be easy, I know." He looks intently into my eyes. "But, I'd walk through the fires of hell for you, Julia. My life's been empty without you. I've been a ghost. I need you more than I need to breathe, more than you need me, beautiful. And I'm man enough to admit it. There's no more half-assing it for me, like before where I expected everything from you. This time, everything is different. You're my forever, my everything, my reason for living. You're my queen."

"There so much that's been left unsaid," I say softly,

trying to get him to see our situation, the impossibility.

He steps closer and gently moves the hair from my face, tracing my face with his fingertips in a loving caress. My eyes close—oh how I've missed his touch. Even at the hardest time in our marriage, he was my hero and I craved his touch. The years have passed, but that hasn't changed the fact that I still crave it and like any addiction, it has the power to destroy me.

"Rome wasn't built in a day and neither will our relationship," he says. My eyes open to look at him once again. "We have to build a strong foundation and rebuild the trust. We were so young when we started and we didn't know how to fix the problems between us. I didn't know how to communicate without showing my fear. I was so busy trying to advance in my career that I drained you and set your dreams aside. I forgot the most important and precious thing in life is family, in doing that, I did you and Kristian wrong. I didn't know what I had until I lost my family."

"How is now any different? Why now, Andre?" My voice rises. "Do you know what seeing you does to me; the pain it causes?"

His eyes close, but not before I see the torture in his eyes.

"You represent everything I've lost. Seeing you, I not only see the man I loved with all my heart but also the man that betrayed me. The man that was angry because I wouldn't give up my dream and conform to the wife he wanted. How am I supposed to overlook everything? Is it fair to me to deal with everything again?" My breathing comes fast with emotion. "I've moved on. I have a life, Andre."

"Really, Julia?" He finally sounds angry. "Do you really

have a life? Because what I've seen is not living. Look at you. Take a look at your life, Julia, and tell me that you're happy. That you wake up every morning with a smile on your face, that the smile you show the world is real, that you sleep peacefully at night, that you're living your dream. Tell me!" He pauses and when I don't answer, he continues. "Tell me that you're happy with your life that you don't crave my touch, my kisses, the way I used to whisper in your ear. Tell me that when you see me, your heart doesn't race, that butterflies don't flutter in your stomach, that the moment you see me, your world isn't right. Because every time I see you, everything is right in my world. I crave you, I need you, and I'll die proving to you that I'm a man that deserves you. When things went to hell for me, you were the only thing that kept me alive. Your memory kept me sane and has driven me to become a man. This time, Julia, I'm not letting you walk away and I'll fight for us. Even if I have to fight for the both of us, I'll fight till my dying breath to show you I deserve you . . ."

Preview Of More Than Forever

More Than Forever

(Book Two, Providence Series)

By: Mary B. Moore

Copyright 2016 to Mary B. Moore

Available Now

LUKE

"LUKE'S RECENT TESTS CONFIRM THAT he does have good brain function. However, the severity of the impact to his brain is keeping him in a coma. How long he's in the coma for? We don't know, but his recent tests are encouraging. Unfortunately, it is just a matter of waiting."

"But, he's been in the coma now for six weeks. His other injuries are almost healed; why can't he just wake up?"

"He will wake up, Christie; he just needs time."

I could hear what they were saying and I wanted to scream that I was here, but my body wasn't letting me. I wanted to open my eyes, but they wouldn't do it. Where was Isla? I needed to see her.

"Look, George, his eyes are opening. Luke, Luke, come on now. Open those eyes for me, please."

The worry in my mom's voice gave me the extra boost to force my eyes open.

"Mr. Montgomery, I'm Doctor Fenwick. How are you feeling? Have you got any pain anywhere?"

I did a quick mental body scan of what I was feeling and where. "My leg," I croaked because that was the area that stood out the most and I just couldn't say more than that right now. Why was I here?

"I'll get you something for that in a minute. I've been looking after you while you recovered from your accident. Now, I'm just going to shine a light in your eyes quickly, I apologize if it's uncomfortable. Can you tell me the last thing you remember, please?"

I tried hard to remember the last thing that happened. I

woke up next to Isla and . . . "Mom, Isla?"

"We'll discuss that later, honey. Can you tell the Doctor the last thing you remember?"

I pushed my brain to bring forward any details that it could.

"Surprise . . . a bang." God, my voice sounded rough, like I'd gargled with a porcupine or something. Suddenly, I saw Maya standing beside me as everything started to fall down around us. "*Maya!*"

And everything went dark.

ISLA

It had been five weeks since I'd arrived in Singapore; the mental image of Luke lying in the hospital bed so broken haunted me. Thinking about that day always made me feel sick, but I was also wondering if I'd picked up some sort of bug or food poisoning a couple of days ago. I felt like death warmed up; my body ached and I couldn't stop being sick.

I missed Luke, I missed Gram, and I missed my boys. Christmas and New Year had been and gone, and the sight of Orchard Road and the rest of Singapore decorated and lit up had been beautiful and breath taking, but it hadn't been the same as it would have been if I'd been with Gram, Reed, Caleb, and Johnny. I couldn't factor Luke and his family into it, like I'd dreamed of being able to do one day.

"Isla, you look beautiful," Dacks said as he leaned in to kiss me on the cheek.

This guy has been my savior since I got here; taking me out, showing me around, and just being amazing in general. It didn't hurt that he was also great to look at.

Blonde hair, tall, dark blue eyes, built . . . if I wasn't so fucked up because of Luke, I might have accepted his date requests, but he'd broken me - again. As if once wasn't bad enough, he did it twice, and the last time was the worst because I thought we had something beautiful; I was wrong.

"Thank you, Dacks, I'm not feeling it, though." I gave a little laugh, trying not to cry as my stomach turned again. "I know we have a lot to do on the Giambini contract, and we've got that meeting with the Deputy Prime Minister next week that we need to prepare for. I'm not feeling so hot today, though, so you'll have to bear with me."

"What's wrong, gorgeous?" He looked so sincere and serious that my eyes started to water. Jesus, I must be ill; I never cry, but I just felt so fricking awful I couldn't help it.

"I think I have a bug or food poisoning," I started to say just as my stomach turned again and my mouth started to fill with that awful water you get just before you throw up.

Jumping up, I ran to the bathroom in the corner of the office and that's when any tiny little molecule of food that could possibly be in my stomach came rushing back up leaving me retching air.

"Here you go," Dacks' deep voice said he held a cold wet towel to my neck. This had to pass and soon; next week was a huge week for the Montgomery's firm, and I refused to let them down.

"Thanks, Dacks. I'll just clean up and be out in a second."

Looking down at the toilet, my stomach twisted again, but I leaned up to flush it and got rid of the mess staring at me without adding to it. As I stumbled to the sink to clean up, I saw Dacks in the mirror standing at the door staring at me. His eyes were flicking between my face and my stomach and he looked worried.

"It's just food poisoning or a bug, Dacks, I'll survive!"

"If you say so," he replied as he turned and walked back over to the desk leaving me wondering what the hell he meant?

LUKE

One week later . . .

Dad had loaded the Singaporean news for me on my iPad so that I could see the moment Isla met with the Deputy Prime Minister. All I wanted to do was see her again and this was the best way. *God, I missed her.*

"The representatives of the Montgomery Corporation, Isla Banks and Dacks Richards, will be meeting with the Deputy Prime Minister today to discuss the building of the Gambini hotel in the Colonial District. The building started three months ago and brought one hundred and ten jobs to Singapore. Once completed, the company has confirmed . . ."

Everyone in the room stopped talking as soon as Isla's name was mentioned and gathered around the bed to watch it with me.

"Ms. Banks is the legal representative from MC and Mr. Richards is the . . ."

I could see them walking up the stairs toward the doors of the building, and I couldn't help feeling pissed that she'd left me. I now knew what Kendal had done and I could guess what lies she told Isla, but she should've waited to talk to me. No, she shouldn't have; I was an asshole, and I'd be surprised if she ever spoke to me again. I should've known that it was a stupid thing to do, but all I'd wanted was for the company to be the international success that it was now becoming. I'd fucked up, though, big time.

I watched the screen as Isla leaned on that bastard Richards who was whispering to her, then Isla suddenly started sinking to the ground and landed on her side on the stair as Dacks quickly reached out for her.

"As you can see, Ms. Banks appears to have fainted. Sources tell us that an ambulance has been called and that her condition at this moment is unknown. We'll update you once we have been informed of Ms. Banks' condition. Also, in the news today - Orchard Road will be . . ."

I didn't want to hear about fucking Orchard Road! Throwing the covers off of my legs, I swung them over the bed to get up. I didn't have the casts anymore, but my leg was still in agony from the severity of the breaks. I needed to toughen up and get to Isla though.

"I'm going to get changed. Call the Doctor and tell him I want to be released today."

Thankfully my mom just nodded and no one challenged my decision as I limped through to the bathroom; it wouldn't have been pretty if they had. This was Isla, for fucks sake!

Preview Of Sugar Baby

SUGAR BABY by Eve Montelibano
Copyrighted © 2016
Coming Soon to Amazon...
THE GAME IS ON...

I feel my pussy gushing more fluids after that brief conversation. I stare at my phone in frustration. He sounded so cold and impersonal. Like he's too busy to be bothered by me.

While you're waiting for him here like his personal whore, excited to feel his touch again. Craving to feel him fill you again. Poor bitch. Where's you game going, I wonder?

I make an unintelligible sound, choking my bitch of a conscience to silence. I don't need to be reminded of that. My swollen, pulsating-with-need kitty is proof enough.

God, three days and I'm craving for him like a druggie. This is the first time he's left me on a business trip for days.

I've been ensconced in his penthouse suite with him most of the month, exploring the joys of carnal ecstasy. I didn't know I already got addicted to his lovemaking. To him. All of him. It happened so quickly and I fully realized it when he left three days ago for Texas.

I hate it. I'm not supposed to feel like this for him. I hate him with every fiber of my being for what he's doing to my father and our family. But I must endure it.

I must be with him for as long as he wishes, until he decides to show mercy and spare my father from going to prison. I'm the sacrificial lamb in an age-old practice of commerce. A bargaining chip.

I have to be thankful the bastard liked me the first time he saw me. I was desperate, grasping at straws.

Two days later, he claimed my virginity. And here I am now, still trying to change his mind.

There's some development though. Dad's trial has been postponed for another three months. Enough for his lawyers to regroup and find other ways to work on a plea bargain.

I knew Josh had something to do with the postponement. I felt it. Nobody can move the trial except the one pushing for it.

I have to build on that hope.

I know I can get my father out of this. I sigh and send Josh another picture.

My phone vibrates.

A message comes in from her again.

I open it and I see her little hand trapped between her tightly crossed legs with the caption: "If you don't come home to scratch this right now, I'll scratch it myself. I've learned new tricks from Xtube. Soon, I won't be needing your cock or any part of you to get me off."

I curse loudly just as the stewardess comes over to tell me the door's open.

I nod at her politely, ignoring the inviting smile on her face, another female willing to be with me for opportunities. I have ceased to believe in the power of my own physical appeal towards the opposite sex since my billions entered the two-digit category. You can't just trust anybody these days.

Whenever a woman approaches me, no matter how decorated her resume is, I'd get a serious case of commitment allergy. I can't help but remember what happened to my buddy Eric when he split with his wife a few years ago. The bitch took half of Eric's hard-earned fortune because the stupid fuck believed in true fucking love he didn't draw a prenup. Talk about blind faith. Even Jesus got betrayed by his disciple and a woman is far from a disciple. I'll never commit that stupid mistake.

I have another great example of that colossal lack of keen character judgment. My grandfather married thrice and all three ended in disaster, the second one nearly bankrupting the Landis coffers as the old man, like Eric, dared to believe in true love. Good thing my father was a genius in numbers and the Landis fortune got replenished over time. Now my father is happily married to his third wife too, but Joshua Junior was wise enough to protect the Landis interests. By the time I was ready to inherit, it has been well inculcated in my skull that marriage is a business deal. It must have an airtight contract attached to it and it must protect my interests first and foremost. Otherwise, no fucking deal.

Now here's the kicker. As much as I hate the idea of shackling myself in matrimony, I'd need one sooner or later to produce a legitimate heir to my fortune. That little brat would serve the purpose as I can demand anything from her and she won't have a choice but to agree or I'll pull the trigger on her father and—

Wow. Seriously?

Shit. That brat makes me think of the stuff I dread like the fucking plague.

Grabbing my attaché case from the nearby seat, I walk towards the exit. The pilot comes out of the cockpit to shake my hand.

"I hope you were able to rest even for a bit during the flight, Mr. Landis," the pilot said with a smile.

"I sure did. Great flying, Grayson. Take a break. Visit your family. I won't be needing you until next week."

"Thank you, Mr. Landis."

I descend the stairs.

My chauffeur is waiting for me a few meters away with the stretch limo.

"Welcome back, Mr. Landis," Floyd, my loyal chauffeur greets me with a slight bow of his capped head.

"Thank you, Floyd. How's everything?"

"All's well and good, sir." I nod.

"Good. Why the limo? I'm alone."

"You might want to relax and take a snooze while we drive towards the city, sir. I stocked the cooler with your favorite drinks and Linda prepared a light snack in there. She figured you'd be hungry by the time you get here. She knows you don't eat on the plane." I smile.

Linda is Floyd's wife and the couple have been in my

employ for ages. They're like family to me, some of the very few people whose loyalty to me has been tested by time.

"I see. Linda knows me too well."

"She sure does. Where to, sir?"

My cock screams home. Now!

"The JL Tower."

I regret it instantly but I won't take it back. My cock must know who's the fucking boss and it's not that fucking pussy.

Floyd nods and opens the limo's door for me. Before I get in, I nod at Reno, my personal bodyguard standing beside a black 4-Runner some meters away, silent as a ghost but deadly.

Reno gave me a salute and boarded the SUV. He will be tailing us, as he does every day if I'm not riding with him.

I enter the limo. Just as Floyd shut the door, a familiar scent attacks my senses like a blitzkrieg. Right there, reclining like a wanton goddess on the black leather seat is my little sexpot.

Clad in an outfit that could have been her old school uniform of white long-sleeved shirt with buttons at the front and a plaid skirt in red and green, her long, honey blond hair in pigtails, she greets me with the kind of smile that has driven men to madness since time immemorial.

"Welcome back, Joshua Landis the Third."

"Cressida, what the fuck are you doing here?"

She craws like a feline on the floor towards me.

"I'm here to welcome you back."

It's obvious, the little brat has taken over my household staff, including my hardcore bodyguard as they all seem to indulge her little whims.

I should send her to the other car, so Reno can drive her back to my apartment and wait for me there like I instructed her to do, but when she puts her hands on my knees and kneels between my legs, I lose the battle with my cock.

I feel myself leaking and I don't think I can attend a meeting in such condition. I wouldn't be able to think straight.

"I told you to wait for me at the apartment."

She makes this little purring sound, like a kitten snuggling closer, seeking body heat. My body heat.

"But I was so sad."

"Why?"

"Because you left me all by my lonesome there."

"I was on a business trip. Besides, you can't miss your classes."

"I was bored out of my panties."

I couldn't hide my smile. The little witch can be funny as shit.

"Bored shopping? Never heard of a female say that."

"You're looking at one."

Her hands creep to my chest, deliberately bypassing my bulging fly. She already knows how to tease me.

"I missed you. The penthouse was so empty without you. Your bed is so huge it made me miss you more."

My cock expands even more, if that's still possible. That girlish lilt in her voice is so sexy and alluring, like a potent drug enhancing my want and need of her.

"Oh Josh, I need you." She breathes, her palms framing my face. They're warm, adding heat to my already over-heating skin.

"Yeah? How much?" I remain calm.

The witch must not know how much I'm dying to bang her right now, like she's the very air that I breathe. She smiles naughtily and her hand dives between her legs and then comes back to my lips.

"Here. Taste how much I want you."

Jesus H! The scent of her arousal invades my nostrils like a snort of coke. Highly addictive shit. My calm goes flying out the window.

Preview Of Hell

HELL

By: Elena M. Reyes

Copyright 2016 to Elena M. Reyes

Available Now

PROLOGUE

WHAT WAS HELL?

If you asked a member of any church today, they'd say it was nightmarish—a dark and gloomy place filled with horrific images and boughs of endless pain. A place where demons roamed freely, feeding off the dregs of the deceased.

A part of humanity that lost its moral compass: the common sinner.

These pour souls sinned in order to achieve greatness; sold their very essence to attain the vanity-filled dreams everyone covets:

Money.

Power.

Respect.

And at the end they'd find themselves with nothing but eternal pain.

Then there were those we called our loved ones. Targeted, they lost the small morsel of their souls that made them good. It made them an easy target.

At the very least, that was what the religious people of the world claimed. Wanted us to believe.

Neither of those descriptions meant shit to me. Religion never mattered much. Not when you'd lost so much and witnessed firsthand just what losing faith did to a person.

I wasn't most people.

Most had chosen to believe the words drilled into their minds from an early age, but I knew better. Hell wasn't somewhere dark where the eternal flames glowed and the sinners were condemned to—to pay for the unforgivable deeds of their past life. Acts that were unforgivable in the eyes of the church.

Stealing.

Killing.

Coveting.

In my reality, though, that was a blatant lie.

Hell was here, surrounding us day in and day out. We paid for our sins in life, not death. One way or another, karma would collect those that wronged another. No one, no matter who the fuck they were, could escape this bitch named life.

Problem was that no matter how much I looked at my

current situation, I was at a loss. What the fuck had I done to deserve *her*?

My hell—the one that tortured me while both awake and asleep—wasn't dark or terrifying. It wasn't painful in the general sense. Well, that was unless you counted the pain my cock had suffered to be life threatening. I guess it could be considered cruel; she loved to torture me when I couldn't react or make her pay.

"You are here to work, not fuck me. My pussy's not on your daily task sheet!"

I'd never been so hard . . .so fucking swollen, as I'd been in her presence. Twitching and pulsating against the zipper of my Levi's, I hurt, and she refused to right the wrong she'd created.

"I don't fuck my employees . . .not even the promising outline of your big cock will change that."

You see, my personal hell was all wrapped up in a lustful package. A body created by God himself, made for the sole purpose of fucking up my quiet and ordinary life. This woman brought me down to my knees—demanded that I pay on a daily basis for the lustful thoughts and impulses she, herself, caused.

"Worry about making sure all the drywall on this floor is up; drilling me isn't on the agenda and never will be."

And I would gladly repent daily, on my knees at her temple, if she would just give in to me.

My version of hell was a woman. A cock tease.

A woman whose inner and outer beauty surpassed the normal standard society had deemed appropriate. Janelle was a temptress, my personal mistress.

Rendered me incapable of both speech and function at

times when all I wanted to do was make her mine. One day Janelle would break me, of that there was no doubt. Problem was that in pushing me past my breaking point, she was losing her power over me and becoming my target. My prey.

When that day came, I would take her without mercy. With no remorse because by then she would be as consumed in her need for me as I was for her.

This woman, angel, or my personal demon, has had my dick hard, leaking and begging for her attention since she first entered my life all those glorious months ago. Now, it was her turn to be miserable.

To feel an eighth of the demands my body made whenever she entered a room. I would make her beg me. Come from a mere look.

Janelle would cry out for me one day, and only then would I gift her my cock.

Her time was up.

I was coming for her.

Preview Of Set Me Free

Set Me Free

(Book One, Free Series)

Copyright 2016 to M.R. Leahy

Available Now

Set Me Free is a dark romance - I do not advise anyone who is sensitive to certain subjects or sexual situations to read it as it does contain certain situations.

Chapter 1
6 years later

Emmalyn

"KODAH, WAKE UP," I WHISPER, shoving the lump in the

bed I call my best friend. "Please, Kodah, wake up!"

"What is it, Emmy?" he asks, his deep voice rough with sleep

"I can hear them screaming, can I please sleep with you?" I beg, wrapping my arms around myself. "I promise I will leave before they come get us."

Usually, the screaming isn't so bad, but one of the new kids mouthed off to a guard today, and now he's paying for it in the room across from ours. Most of the time the guards just take them to the main house, but sometimes, like this time, they like to remind us of the consequences of getting out of line. You learn quickly to keep your mouth shut and do as your told unless you want to die, or worse, get passed around to a bunch of psychotic guards whose only entertainment is when a kid misbehaves.

Scooting over, Kodah pulls the covers back, gesturing for me to lie next to him. "Come here."

Crawling under the covers, he pulls me up against his chest and wraps his arms around me. I let out a sigh and snuggle back into the safety of his arms, this is my safe place.

It has been five years since my dad gave me up to my mom and left me to live in this hell with her new husband, who happens to be the ring leader of this whole establishment. Being the daughter of the owners you would think I would have some sort of immunity to what goes on around here, but I don't, not even close. I was told from the beginning that my purpose here is greater than all the other kids. I was going to be the example. I guess it has to do with image, because if a person is willing to torture and sell their own child, imagine what they will do to someone who isn't theirs. It's a form of power, at least that's what I'm told. The objective is that once I turn sixteen, I am going to be sold to the highest bidder, something I have been training for since the day I arrived. If you can even call what I am put through training.

You see, as soon as a kid arrives at this godforsaken place—whether they were kidnapped, bought, or used to pay off a debt—you are automatically put into a group of traits. Those traits consist of farmers, indoor and outdoor laborers, servants, and, of course, sex slaves, just to name a few. Some are even put into more than one group like Kodah. Because he's great with his hands, strong, and very good looking, he's forced to train to be a farmer, indoor and outdoor laborer, and a sex slave.

Me? I only have one purpose here, and that is to be the best submissive sex slave money can buy. Unfortunately for me, my sixteenth birthday was yesterday. As much as I hate this place, I would much rather stay here where at least I know the rules and what is expected of me then be sold to some sick sadist who will do God-only-knows-what to me.

Kodah has been stuck in this place since he was eight and is the oldest kid here. It's very rare for a nineteen-year-old to still be here, especially one as good looking and as talented as he's. Most kids are either sold or killed by the time they're seventeen.

He doesn't talk about it much; all I know is that he was payment for a debt his parents owed and even at eight years old, he came here with so much rage that he had to be sedated for several days. But that's Kodah for you. In the five years I have been here I have seen him beaten, whipped, chained, and taken away to entertain more times than I'd like to count, and each time, it never changed a thing. If anything, it just made him fight harder, and they never killed him because they didn't like to waste such potential. It wasn't until I was the one chained and whipped for his defiance that he started to actually obey and take his training seriously.

Since the beginning, Kodah and I have had a special type of connection that can't be explained with words. We have always been each other's safe place. He has taught me how to protect myself, removing my mind from situations that could mentally destroy me. He has shown me how to find a safe place within myself when things around me are anything but.

Once upon a time, my safe place had been my father. He, my brother, and my uncles were my everything, I was treated like a princess among rough and scary men, and I had never wanted that to change. Then just like that, it did, just a few nights before my tenth birthday, my mom had shown up while my dad and uncles had gone on a run for business, or so they had said. My mom had told me that they had left because they didn't want to say goodbye to me. Apparently, business for my dad was getting to be too much for a man in his position, and he didn't have time to raise a daughter, so he gave me away.

Just like that, my world was turned upside down. Now I am a slave like all these other kids and trained to become whatever our buyers want us to be.

"Kodah, do you miss your parents?" I ask, staring into the dark

"No, I don't even remember them," he replies, his tone dismissive

I wish I didn't remember my family. I guess that's the hardest part—the memories. I have nothing but good memories of my family, that's why it was so hard when I found out they never had wanted me. Reaching for my necklace, I grab the little gold heart that dangles from the delicate chain. It is the only thing I have to remind me of my dad. He had given it to me as a birthday present the night my mom came to get me. He used to tell me to hold on to my heart, to always protect it, to never give it away for free, and to always cherish it. The world was full of evil people who would do anything to take advantage of a heart so pure. He bought me the necklace as a reminder to never forget the pureness in myself when the world threatened to take it away. Little did I know that I was about to see how impure the world really was.

Shaking off the memory, I roll over and put my face into his bare chest inhaling the smell of soap and sunshine, a smell you only get when you spend the majority of your life working in the sun, that was all Kodah.

"What is it, Emmy? What's really bothering you?" he asks, always able to read me. Pulling back, he looks me in the eyes. Kodah Mason is what dreams are made out of; his tan skin that has light freckles covering it from the sun brings out the blue in his eyes almost making them glow. His dark hair is kept short like all the rest of the boys here. He's tall and muscular from all the labor and strict diet they have him on. He's complete perfection. It's a true mystery why he hasn't been bought yet, regardless of his attitude. Whatever the reason, I am just glad he's still here, as selfish as that sounds, he's the only reason I have to get up every day. Without him, I would be lost.

Letting out a breath I didn't realize I was holding, I answer him, "My mom came to visit me today." Feeling him tense, I continue. "She said that they will be having guests arriving soon and I am going to be the entertainment."

Unwrapping his arms from me, he sits up, leaning against the wall, taking his comfort with him. Leaving me feeling the dread of what's to come.

Every once in a while, Marx will hold a "dinner" where he invites all of his acquaintances that mostly consist of buyers, and gives them a dinner and a show.

Training to be a sex slave is bad enough, but having to perform in front of a bunch of hungry, sadistic men is a different type of torture. They basically take everything you have learned and put on a show. I compare these events to the ballet recitals I did as a little girl, only instead of pink tutus and calming music, you're naked, and it's the sounds of whips and chains.

"Why do you have to perform? They only let the kids who are ready to be sold do that."

Unable to lie there anymore, I sit up, pulling my knees to my chest and face him. "It probably has to do with the fact that I turned sixteen yesterday. He probably wants to make sure I'm ready. The reason doesn't even matter, there's nothing I can do about it anyway."

The look of sadness that crosses his face at the mention of my birthday, has me regretting my words. Every year that goes by in this place, is just another year of hopeful wishes and dreams lost and forgotten. Every birthday that has gone by has brought us closer to this moment, it became a day of dread, and he hates that.

Hearing a loud scream, we both look at the door. Poor kid. For his sake, I hope he dies soon. Death would be better than what he's going through.

Shaking his head, he turns and looks at me, desperation in his eyes. "We have to do something. You don't want to perform, Emmy, trust me. They're going to take everything you have learned and amplify it, making you really fucking work. You are going to be the slave he wants to sell. No training, just obeying, and if you fuck up, they will beat the shit out of you . . . or worse."

My body starts trembling, and I shake my head. "You don't think I don't know this," I hiss, not wanting to raise my voice. "I remember every single time they had to drag you back in here after you had to perform, I remember the ghosts that haunted you . . . that still haunt you. But what can I do about it? Huh? Nothing. All I can do is turn my mind off and hope I don't fuck this up," I say through clenched teeth, trying to hold back the emotions that threaten to consume me.

Grabbing my leg, he pulls it over him, causing me to land in his lap, both my legs on either side of his and our chests nearly touching.

"Shh, baby, I got you," he murmurs, running his hands up and down my back as he pulls me in as close as I can get, my body pressing against his, the safety of his embrace causing my trembling to slowly stop. "When is this happening?"

"Three days," I whisper back, tucking my face into the crook of his neck. I just want to forget what is coming.

"I'll figure this out, Emmy, OK? I'm not going to just stand by and let you go through with this; I have to try to do something."

Kodah and I have a bond that's unbreakable. It was more than love at first sight for us—it was a recognition so deep that we never once questioned what could or couldn't be between us, only what has been and what was going to be. Six years of sharing a room together in a place that threatens to steal every ounce of light from you, we have held each other up, we keep each other going, but other times, we have been each other's weakness.

Feeling his fingers tangle in my hair, I sigh as he pulls my head back. Looking up into his eyes, I feel my body heat as I recognize the look he's giving me.

With hooded eyes, he leans in and whispers as if he's in pain, "Just one, Emmy, and then you need to get some sleep."

Licking my suddenly dry lips, I nod, unable to speak.

Leaning the rest of the way in, he brushes his lips against mine, causing my eyes to flutter close and my body to melt against his. Feeling my body respond, he pulls my hair more causing me to gasp. Taking full advantage, he deepens the kiss, swiping his tongue against mine.

Feeling my mind give way to my body, I grip the side of his shirt and rock my body against his, seeking some sort of relief, drawing a growl from his chest. But as soon as I feel like we are finally getting somewhere, I sense him slowing down, and with one last peck on my lips, he pulls back.

The blue of his eyes is almost taken over by the black of his pupil, his heavy breaths fanning my face. "You should probably head to bed, baby," he says, his voice thick with lust

Other than holding each other at night and a couple touches here and there, this is the most contact we ever have, not because we don't want more, but with the invasive monthly exams I get to make sure everything is still intact, we literally can't. We also have this want that the first time we do anything we don't want it tainted by this ugly place. That doesn't mean things haven't gotten out of hand before, it just means that one of us usually comes to our senses before things can go too far.

Sighing, I look across the room at my little bed.

All the rooms are the same, about the size of a walk-in closet that can fit two very small beds with a table that sits next to each bed and an adjoined bathroom that is so small if you put your arms out you can touch each wall. I have been told by kids who came here from other slave rings that this place is paradise. I guess that would be why my step-father is one of the top in his trait and has yet to be caught. We are all fed properly and well-groomed, we are taken care of as far as our health goes, none of us drugged out, and as long as we learn quickly and do as we are told, we don't get beaten or killed. Sure, the guards get handsy, and deaths happen regularly, but what do you expect in a place like this? Marx Nixon is always saying that in order for him to be the best, he has to sell the best. So, in other words, he has established a legitimate child slavery trade.

Nodding, I turn back to him. "OK, Kodah, goodnight."

"Goodnight, Emmy."

More Authors To Check Out

These are just a few of my favorite authors, that are automatic one click for me, for you to check out. The ones with the * by them appear in this book you just read

ML Rodriguez*
Mary B Moore*
C.M. Steele*
Elena M. Reyes*
Eve Monte
KC Lynn*
K. Langston*
Cassia Brightmore*
Sarah Curtis
Winter Travers
M.R. Leahy
Brynne Ashers
Layla Frost
Jess Eeps
Sarah O'Rourke
Trinity Rose

76257258R00177

Made in the USA
Columbia, SC
04 September 2017